Where the Dance Is

Praise for *When Memory Dies*

'Haunting, with an immense tenderness. The extraordinary
poetic tact of this book makes it unforgettable'
– John Berger, *Guardian*

'A brilliant and moving first novel. With a grandeur reminiscent
of the great Indonesian novelist, Pramoedya Ananta Toer,
Sivanandan takes the reader through three generations of a
Sri Lankan family. As we move from the days of the *hartal*
in 1920 through independence in 1948 to the neo-liberal
pangs of the 1980s, Sri Lankan communalism gathers force
like a conquering flood' – *Times Literary Supplement*

'This is not just a book about Sri Lanka. The struggles it
touches upon, both moral and political, face us all: the battle
between our hunger for love or learning or success and our
need, even passion, for integrity. This is a book of, and about,
many lifetimes' – Melissa Benn, *Independent*

'This rich novel, peopled with unforgettable heroines and
heroes, will haunt the reader's mind' – David Rose, *Observer*

'Profoundly moving. Sivanandan triumphs in his evocation of a
beautiful country he perceives as doomed. His love for the
country he has lost is the driving passion for his work'
– *Evening Standard*

'There is no rallying cry here, no dwelling on the tragedies of
the individual, only an exhortation to memory and constant
effort. Sivanandan's sensibilities and instincts are endlessly
humane, generous and perceptive' – *Literary Review*

Where the Dance Is

Stories from Two Worlds and Three

A. Sivanandan

A

ARCADIA BOOKS

LONDON

Arcadia Books Ltd
15–16 Nassau Street
London w1n 7re

www.arcadiabooks.co.uk

First published in Great Britain by Arcadia Books 2000
Copyright © A. Sivanandan 2000

A. Sivanandan has asserted his moral right
to be identified as the author of this work in accordance with the
Copyright, Designs and Patents Act, 1988.

All Rights Reserved. No part of this publication
may be reproduced in any form or by any means
without the written permission of the publishers.

A catalogue record for this book is available
from the British Library.

isbn 1–900850–19–2

Typeset in Stempel Garamond by Discript, London wc2n 4bl
Printed in the United Kingdom by The Cromwell Press, Trowbridge, Wiltshire

Published with financial support of the London Arts Board

Arcadia Books distributors are as follows:

in the UK and elsewhere in Europe:
Turnaround Publishers Services
Unit 3, Olympia Trading Estate
Coburg Road
London n22 6tz

in the USA and Canada:
Consortium Book Sales and Distribution, Inc.
1045 Westgate Drive
St Paul, MN 55114–1065

in Australia:
Tower Books
PO Box 213
Brookvale, NSW 2100

in New Zealand:
Addenda
Box 78224
Grey Lynn
Auckland

in South Africa:
Peter Hyde Associates (Pty) Ltd
PO Box 2856
Cape Town 8000

BCA

CROYDON PUBLIC LIBRARIES

Lib. LNI   No. 434 8672

Class   F

V OWBC   P £10.99

Stk.   2|5|01

Contents

... at the still point, there the dance is ...

T. S. Eliot

The Performer

He was my teacher. Or, rather, he taught at the Catholic school I once attended — a flamboyant man, not in dress or manners, like Archie Ratnam (he did not, for instance, tuck a silk handkerchief in his sleeve) but in his personal style, flamboyant in the sense of calling attention to himself, and doing it through his personality.

He laughed, and all the world laughed with him. It was hearty, loud, reverberating through the world and enveloping it — enveloping but not embracing it, for he was, somehow, outside it all. It was *his* laugh, though. He began it well before the world was ready for it, and the world was inexplicably caught out of step. And, lost out in its timing, it guiltily joined in, the more heartily for having not anticipated it in the first place.

A good fellow, a merry fellow, a sharp, sharp fellow, very incisive, perceptive. Else, why were we always caught short, always lagging behind him, and not just his laughter. Those sudden darts he made from one subject to another, connecting them in the end, if only with some witticism, some *risqué* joke, anecdote or just with that huge big self-confident laugh of his.

He would come into a room, into the clubhouse, step out into the garden, leap out of a car, and the world around him would stop moving on its own axis and say, shame-facedly, 'ah, here's Walter,' and then proceed to revolve around him.

Or he would be serious – political, analytical. He took the world apart, showed you what was wrong with it, told you how he would put it together. Economics, law, politics, agriculture, plantations, industry, coconut-growing, copra-manufacturing, Roman-Dutch law, NATO and SEATO and India and China – he had answers for them all.

And we believed him. We believed in his affairs too, more than he ever did. There were a number of them, many at the same time, but they were essentially satellite affairs surrounding the one big love of his life. His grand amour had lasted these twenty years. He wore it like a bleeding heart, but not so as you would notice it, he brandished it like a poniard, but with the point turned towards him. Every so often he would cede her to her husband, with the humility of a man who knew he did not deserve her.

Nor could we blame him. Kumari was majestic. Tall and dark, with a figure rounding nicely, but firmly, into her thirties, she carried herself with the grace of the Kathakali dancer that she once was. There was a stillness about her, like the still point of the dancing world, that one was loath to break. Even Walter, who was all chatter, was tongue-tied in her company. Kumari liked him for that, liked his silences and gave no heed to his reputation for garrulity. It was, in fact, Nimal, her husband, who did most of the talking when they got together, mostly on dance nights at the 20-20

Club of which they were members.

Walter invariably arrived without a partner – not daring to parade his affairs before Kumari – and ended up dancing with her. Nimal did not mind. A good dancer himself, he could only admire the way that his wife and Walter melded together on the dance floor, especially in the tango. Something came over Walter then: that stillness that only Kumari had seen up till now, the same stillness in motion that Kumari possessed – and a stillness from motion, as they stood poised, statuesque, for the music to commence. Everybody left the floor, as though by common consent, and waited for the dance to explode into the erotic sensuality of passion unspoken, only to find that the purity and grace of line and movement had transported them to another world of the senses where the only truth that mattered was beauty. And a wave of regret would pass over Nimal that he had taken Kumari from Walter, her childhood sweetheart.

Kumari and Walter had grown up together in a south Colombo tenement. Walter's father was the head cook at St Ignatius' College and personal chef to the Rector, Father La Fontaine, a Frenchman of fierce integrity whose only weakness was his penchant for Ceylonese cuisine. It was through that chink in his 'armour palate', Joseph Perera would confide to his friends, that he had managed to get his son into the prestigious boarding-school without entrance exam or fee. It helped, of course, that Joseph was a devout Catholic and his son a good looking choir-boy, with his mother's angelic features. But according to Mary, whose bluntness belied her looks, it was her husband's willingness to sacrifice their son to the priesthood that had made all the difference.

Kumari's parents were basket-weavers and, although they lived only two doors below the Pereras, Joseph had enjoined his family not to get too close to people who were not in proper employment. He was a bit of a snob and was always seeking the approval of his betters, but he was a kind man, and neither his wife nor his son took any notice of his strictures, of which, Mary was sure, her husband was secretly ashamed. Kumari, besides, was the closest thing to the daughter Mary never had, and Suman, Kumari's brother, was her son's best friend. The children went freely in and out of each others' houses, only the parents remained aloof.

Walter and Kumari were the same age and Suman a year older. But it was Kumari who led them in the adventures in the junk-yard behind the tenements. She was vivacious and outgoing, with bright sparkling eyes and an iron will and already, at seven, had the boys giving in to her every whim. Walter was her particular devotee. Shy and sensitive himself, he saw in Kumari the sort of person he would have liked to be, but it was Suman he was comfortable with.

They were all bright children and did well at the state school they attended. Suman was the most studious of the three and, by the time he was fourteen years old, had won a scholarship to Anuradha College, the premier Buddhist school in the capital. It was then that Joseph, mortified that a basket-weaver's son should upstage his own, had gone to Father La Fontaine and offered his son to the seminary.

Kumari felt robbed. She had already married Walter in a solemn ceremony of their own when they were nine years old. Every year on their birthday — they were born on the same day in the same year and took it to be an omen — they renewed their marriage vows and swore to be faithful to each other for ever more. But now it looked as though Walter was going to become a priest and would never be able to marry her.

'What are we going to do?' she asked Walter, when he broke the news to her in their secret lair under the hood of a disused Chevrolet in the junk-yard.

'Run away?' offered Walter, expecting that that was what Kumari would want him to say.

'Don't be silly. We are too young for that sort of thing,' replied Kumari tetchily. 'Why can't you go to day school like Suman?'

'Then I won't be a seminarian.'

'H'm, that is true.' She twisted and untwisted her plait. 'But you don't want to be a priest?'

'No, but then I can't go to college.'

Kumari was defeated by the logic of it all for a minute, and then came up with the solution.

'So, don't.'

'Don't? Don't go to school? At all?'

'You mean our school is not good enough for your father?'

'It isn't, is it? And I am not as clever as Suman, to do what he did.' He thought about that for a moment. 'No, I am not. It has all been arranged, anyway. I start next term.'

Kumari turned away to hide her tears. Walter instinctively wrapped his arms around her, and hurriedly took them away again.

'Kumari, you've got...' he stammered.

'Why, what did you think I was? A boy?' She rounded angrily on Water and, crying, ran from him.

Walter started to go after her and stopped. 'What did I say?' he asked himself miserably, sitting on the trunk of a fallen tree. The last thing he wanted to do was to hurt Kumari. She and Suman were the people he loved most in the world, next to his parents. But what could he do? He hated going to a new school, let alone being boarded, and he never wanted to be a seminarian. Why couldn't grown-ups leave things as they were? Tears began to well up in his eyes.

'Walter?' He felt a hand on his shoulder and, looking up, saw Suman standing over him. 'Are you all right?' There was so much concern in his voice that Walter burst out crying. 'What's the matter?' Suman sat down beside his friend and wiped away his tears. But his hands were so gentle that Walter began to cry again. 'It's Kumari, isn't it?' Walter nodded. 'Because you are going away?' Walter nodded again.

'I don't want to become a priest and I don't want to hurt her.'

'Oh, girls get over these things, you know,' Suman comforted his friend, with the wisdom of his elderhood. There was only a year between them, but Suman's voice had already broken and a wisp of hair had begun to adorn his upper lip. 'She is bound to find someone else.'

That made Walter even more unhappy.

'I know what,' laughed Suman, 'you can always chuck up the seminary, or get them to chuck you.'

'Yes. I can do that, can't I?' Walter cheered up.

'That's settled then. Let's go and tell Kumari,' and he took Walter by the hand.

But Kumari would have none of it. She had got over her disappointment, she told Walter grandly, and had no reason to trust him ever again – not unless he gave her a promise in writing that he would never become a priest and would return to her one day. Suman was to be witness and guarantor.

Four years later, Walter left the seminary, but not of his own volition. His father had died the year before in suspicious circumstances and the Church refused to let him be buried on consecrated land. The rumour was that Joseph was not really the devout Catholic and devoted husband everyone thought him to be, but a gambler and womanizer who had died at the hands of a jealous husband. Joseph had apparently been robbing the College blind for years to pay off his gambling debts and provide for his mistress and her two children. It was only when Father Fernando succeeded old Father La Fontaine as Rector of the College that Joseph's misdemeanours came to light.

As the first Ceylonese Rector of St Ignatius' College, the Reverend Isidore Fernando was anxious to prove to the Church that he could save the College from the financial waste and moral decline into which it had drifted during the lax regime of his more scholarly and unworldly predecessor, and he set about his mission with the moralistic fervour of the accountant turned ascetic. Himself a tall, thin wafer of a man, with little time for food and even less for cooks and their cuisines, his first port of call was the College kitchen (boarders and priestlings, he held, should do with basic rations) and his first victim the College cook. Sound accountant that he was, Father Fernando did not sack old Joseph on the spot, but allowed him to stay on and pay for his sins, venal and carnal, under threat of excommunication, with drastic cuts in his wages. Unable to fend for his wife, let alone his mistress and her children, to support whom he had taken to stealing and gambling, Joseph took his life.

That, anyway, was Father Fernando's version of events and, suicide being a mortal sin, the Church had no choice, it declared, but to refuse Joseph a Christian burial.

Walter was desolated. He knew his father was a good man. Everybody knew that, till the Church told them otherwise and they began to change their minds. Stealing? What stealing? Everybody knew that his father often took food from the kitchen and gave it to the children in the slums on his way home, and everybody had liked him for it. And the woman who was supposed to be his mistress was his wife Mary's cousin, Alice, who had been beaten and abused by her stepfather for years till her mother found out and threw her and her children out on the streets; it was Mary who had prevailed on her husband to care for them. Everybody knew about that too and expected that he had slept with Alice. But they took their cue from Mary who knew that her husband could not separate the caring from the loving, and the loving from the making love, and had still wanted him to husband them. After all, he took nothing away from her.

Walter had gone with his father to visit cousin Alice and her children in their make-shift shed on a few occasions, and he had always come away ashamed that he did not love his father as unquestioningly as they did.

It was the gambling Walter was not sure about. He knew his father liked to play *buruwa* with his mates at work, but, declared his mother, the stakes were never very high and the occasions infrequent.

'It is that fellow Fernando,' she said dismissively, 'he made it all up.' She was pounding the husk from the paddy as she was speaking and, with every sentence, the pounding got fiercer. 'Father he calls himself. Ha. He has never fathered a living thing in his life, the desiccated little bugger.'

His mother's anger was a joy to watch, so seldom did it erupt, but when it did, it flowed like molten lava. It affected Walter deeply and ignited some of his own anger against the Church. Not that he did not like his life in the seminary: there was an uninhibited affection and fellowship among the boys that made up for the rigour and ritual of monastic life. He was even beginning to like the discipline. But, underneath it all, he could not help feeling, there was something fundamentally dishonest about the Church. It all stemmed from the time when Suman used to come to visit him and was treated by Walter's seminarian friends as someone who did not quite belong there, with them, the chosen. Which was when Walter began to notice that non-Catholics were kept out of the College cricket and football teams and from its more prestigious events. And, somewhere along the line, he began to feel that the Church did not practise the universal love it preached.

'He made it all up, all right, but not from nothing,' Walter heard his mother say.

'Who?'

'Father bloody Fernando, that's who.' She stopped pounding the paddy and, setting herself down on her haunches, pulled out her pouch of betel leaves and are-canut from the folds of her sari. Walter sat down on the cool stone floor before her.

'He made it all up from the facts that your father left lying around and made them into a huge lie. But the facts were there, you see. So they were ready to believe anything that damn Church said. Too open he was your father, too innocent.'

Mary folded the betel leaf and bits of arecanut into a sizeable chew and put it in her mouth while Walter was still marvelling at her effrontery. He had always suspected that his mother was sceptical about the Church, if not her religion, and had gone along to mass and benediction just to please his father. But he had never thought of her as a rebel. Perhaps his father's death had released her, perhaps he himself had never seen her before.

'What's the matter? Have you never seen me chewing betel?'

Walter shrugged the question aside and wanted to

know when his father had begun to fall ill. Was it when his friends . . .

Mary nodded and went on chewing. 'You came home in August. What, two months before he died? He was bad then. His friends had stopped coming. They were afraid the Church . . . That broke his heart. I could do nothing, nothing. And I was going downhill. Trying to keep him up. But that boy, Suman. He used to come round. Great help he was. Kumari had gone to that dance school. He put on a brave face for you, your father. He wanted you to become a priest. Save his soul.' She began to cry softly.

'Did he take his life, mother?' asked Walter after a while.

'No, son, he just died. He had had enough. He did not want to live. Even for me. The Church, his friends. They were his life.'

She wiped the tears resolutely from her eyes and, going up to the kitchen door, spat out a stream of betel juice as red as blood. 'You had better leave that damn seminary. I only wanted you to go there for your education. It's too late to save your father. The only problem is how to pay for your teacher training.' She thought for a moment, weighing the odds. 'But you don't want to be a priest, do you?'

Walter went up to his mother and embraced her gratefully. 'That's what I came home to tell you, but I was not sure how you'd take it.' He released his mother and went and sat down on a chair by the kitchen table.

'Tell me what?'

'I don't have to leave, mother, they have sacked me,' replied Walter and, seeing the look of disbelief on Mary's face, went on to tell her how Father Fernando had persuaded him that the stigma of his father's suicide would inevitably attach to him and affect his work as a priest. The fact that he was going to be a teacher-priest instead of a parish priest might make it less public, but in the end a priest was a priest. The Church, of course, would not dream of sacking him – 'the sins of the father' notwithstanding – but if Walter himself decided to leave, without a fuss, Father Fernando would see to it that his future at Teacher Training College was not 'interrupted'.

'That's it then, the bastards,' Mary was angry and relieved in turn. 'When do you come home?'

'In three weeks, for Christmas – for good. Then in January next year, I go to Training College.'

'That's when our girl is coming home.'

'Our girl? Oh, you mean –'

'Yes, Kumari,' she smiled archly, and went back to winnowing the rice.

'Mother!' he reproved her, 'I am hardly out of the seminary, and here you are...' He paused. It was just beginning to dawn on him that he was a free man. It would be good to see Kumari again, properly.

He had not seen much of her on his occasional visits in the past few years. He had written her a clandestine note on their first birthday apart, renewing his vow to marry her. And although he had not expected her to reply – all his letters had to be 'passed' by the head priest – he had assumed that her feelings towards him had not changed. But when he saw her a year later, she seemed reluctant to talk about their relationship, and he did not feel he had the right to broach the subject. Besides, she was already, at sixteen, growing into a beautiful, self-possessed woman, and he did not dare approach her with the same insouciance as before. Then, last year, she had been discovered in a dance-drama version of the *Mahabharata*, put on by her school in the National Schools' Drama Competition, and been admitted to Nanda Sena's Dance Academy. Walter had not seen her since,

'Why don't you go and see Suman and tell him the good news?' His mother broke into his reverie.

'H'm, that's a good idea. Is he at home?'

'I saw him this morning,' she replied, but he was already out of the room. 'Put on a shirt,' she called after him.

Walter picked up a shirt on the way out and worked himself into it. It was his father's and it was too small for him. He had suddenly shot up in the last year and was now only a couple of inches short of Suman's six feet.

Suman was hanging up the washing on a makeshift line in their tiny compound when Walter came into view.

'Mother,' he called, 'look who's here. It's the padre . . . Good Lord, he's almost as tall as me.'

Chandra Herath came out and embraced Walter. Bent and arthritic, she reached up to his chest, 'You are right. He has grown.' She released him and held him at arm's length. 'How are you son?' she asked anxiously, remembering how badly he had taken his father's death. She and her husband had stood by Joseph when all his friends had left him, but Herath himself had died of a heart attack a week before Joseph passed away.

'I am fine, aunty. I've left the seminary.' He said it casually, calmly, hoping to arouse their curiosity, but was taken aback when mother and son cried out in unison: 'Oh great. Well done.'

'They kicked me out, really,' Walter corrected himself, and told them what had happened.

Chandra was not surprised. She had seen how Joseph had struggled to hold on to the Church even as the Church was leaving him. She did not expect it to treat Walter any better. But Suman could not hide his pleasure and, when his mother had gone into the house to make the tea, took Walter aside and reminded him of their conversation all those years ago.

'But I never thought it would happen like this,' remonstrated Walter.

'What does it matter how it comes about. It has. Aren't you glad?'

Walter thought about that for a while, squatting against the wall of the house and trying to keep the sun from his eyes.

'Yes and no, Suman,' he said with great deliberation. 'Yes, I was never cut out to be a priest. But no. I should have had the strength to leave of my own accord. You see, I have no convictions. Unlike you.' Suman tried to protest, but Walter held up his hand. 'Let me go on, while it's still in my head.'

Suman up-ended the wash bucket and sat on it.

'Here you are,' continued Walter, 'half-way through your first year in the University and you are already secretary of the Young Socialists' League. You know where you are going. I don't. You know who you are. I don't. I don't even know who I'm allowed to love any more.'

'Kumari?'

'I don't know. I couldn't ask myself that question up to now.' He scratched his head. 'And she has changed so much. Hasn't she?'

'If you mean, is she still a tom-boy, certainly not. She has grown out of all that and become quieter, and more contained. But her affections have not changed, I don't think,' and then, as an afterthought, he added that Walter had changed too, and not just physically.

'Have I?' Walter was curious.

'Oh, yes. You'd never have talked so openly to me like this in the past. You were so shy and reserved. You are just the opposite now.'

'Loud and brash, you mean,' Walter smiled wryly. 'No, I'm not, not really. I just put it on to cover my real feelings – not with you, of course. It's the one thing I learnt to do in the seminary.' He picked up a stick and absent-mindedly drew patterns on the ground. 'I seem to be acting all the time, and I don't know which act is me.'

❧

That December, the monsoon was heavy and unrelenting. It drove through the tenements in waves of torrential rain, lifting the roofs of the houses on the high ground and flooding the ones below. Mary's and

Chandra's houses which lay between escaped the worst of the damage. But just as the monsoon was blowing itself out, a freak gust of wind took the tiles off a side of Chandra's roof, leaving a gaping hole over the kitchen. Suman tried to cover it up before the next rain with a thin sheet of tin, held down by bricks, but it kept sliding off. He was wondering what he could do to hold it down when Walter turned up.

'Why didn't you call me?' he reproached Suman. 'If my mother hadn't seen you on the ladder and told me —'

'I thought I could manage. Hand me those bricks.'

'I don't think that's going to work, Suman. What we need is a tarpaulin which we can tie down at the corners.'

'Where from?'

'That junk-yard owner, Banda, has a couple. I am sure I saw —'

'I'll go and ask him,' called out a voice from within.

'When did she arrive?' asked Walter.

'She came this morning,' replied Kumari, emerging from the house in an old windcheater and cap. 'Hello, Walter.'

'Hello sailor,' Walter greeted her warmly.

'Ha-hah, the same old Walter with the same old dry jokes. Come on,' and she took him by the arm, 'let's get that tarpaulin before it starts raining again.'

The following day, the monsoon ceased as suddenly as it had arrived, and the sun blazed down on the muddy earth and set it in furrow. Walter and Kumari went in search of their Chev in the junk-yard, but found the place tidied up beyond recognition. Only the old jak tree was still there where it had fallen, and they sat on its bole, recalling their childhood adventures.

'You are not so bossy now,' observed Walter.

'And you are not so sheepish,' came the riposte.

They laughed and held hands and looked into each other's eyes – and were reassured.

'Was there anyone...' Walter began tentatively.

'For a short while, yes,' replied Kumari, and fell silent. Walter did not press her.

She released his hand and stared vacantly into the distance. When she spoke again, it was with a strange mixture of wistfulness and denial. His name was Nimal, she told Walter. He was Nanda Sena's son and he danced with the troupe. But he wanted to be a lawyer. He did it for his father, the dancing. She hesitated, not sure how Walter was taking her revelations. It hadn't lasted that long, though, she reassured Walter, the affair – two months, if that, before he went off to law college in Colombo. She was still training in Kerala at the time.

She stole a look at Walter, at his innocent face and, remembering how he never passed judgement on her, took his hands in hers and began to unburden herself. Nimal, with his snub nose and frizzy hair, was nowhere near as good-looking as Walter, she said. Yet, there was an intensity about him that dazzled you like beauty. She had been fascinated by him, had given into him, given herself up to him, discovered an answering passion in herself no less fierce than his.

But when they finally broke up, she felt consumed. For months, all she could think of was how Walter would have loved her, preserved her, even against herself.

Walter was shocked and anxious, and solicitous and mollified in turn – and, for once, his emotions showed on his face.

'I am sorry, Walter, but you are my best friend and my best love, and I had to tell you who I am.'

'I know,' said Walter and turned to kiss her cheek, but she moved her face, catching him on the mouth, and lingered there. Walter blushed, it was his first proper kiss.

Walter saw little of Kumari after that, as she was either touring with her troupe in the regions or learning new dance forms in India. He wrote to her regularly, but received only the occasional note in reply; she was, she confessed, a congenitally bad correspondent. But she made up for it on her visits home when she spent all her time with Walter. And it was generally assumed that they would be married as soon as Walter got through his exams and became a teacher.

Spurred on by that prospect, Walter threw himself into his studies and, with Suman's help in the subjects common to them both, came top of his class in the first two years. Then, six months before his finals, Kumari's letters became less frequent, showed less urgency, and finally ceased altogether. Walter flagged, and ended up with a mere pass. Luckily for him, the new Rector at St Ignatius' wanted Walter back in his school as a teacher, whether to redress past wrongs or because of Walter's showing as a trainee teacher, Walter was not sure. Nor did he wish to find out. All that mattered to him was that his future was secure, and he made that doubly certain within a year when, urged on by Kumari who had started writing again, he sat an external honours degree from London University and passed with an upper second. He was promptly promoted to the Senior School to teach the university entrance classes, with a substantial rise in pay. He wrote at once to Kumari asking her to set a date, and was beginning to make wedding plans when he received a telegram from her – through Suman.

It was a cool January morning, the dew still on the grass at seven o'clock: the sun was late coming. Walter remembered it well.

His mother was in bed with a fever and he was taking her a cup of tea when Suman arrived at the kitchen door, a red envelope in his hand.

'She's set a date, has she?' piped up Walter cheerfully. 'Agreed to become a Catholic?' and, seeing Suman's long face, 'wants you to become a Catholic? Me to become a Buddhist...' He trailed off. 'What's the matter?'

'She's gone, Walter. Married. To that guy Nimal.'

'You are joking ... No you are not ... Nimal? Nimal!' The cup fell from his hands and shattered into a hundred fragments on the stone floor. He went down on his knees, picking up the pieces, crying under his breath, calling out her name. Suman picked up the pieces with him.

Walter made another cup of tea and took it in to his mother. He was back a moment later.

'She's sound asleep,' he said, putting the cup back

on the table and joining Suman on the kitchen step.
'Why did she wire you and not me?'

'I don't know. Feeling guilty.'

'About what?'

'Maybe, she had to get married.'

'Pregnant, you mean?' Suman nodded. Walter threw
up his hands in despair: he had heard everything now.

'And she probably thought I should be with you
when you received the news.'

Walter began to cry again and Suman reached out
and wiped his tears. Walter took his hand. 'There was
another time when you —'

'Yes, I know.'

'You are a good friend, Suman.' Walter hugged him.
'You are always there, when I need you. With your
help, I dare say I'll get over this too.'

But Walter never got over his hurt. He covered it
up instead, put a face on it, played the man of the
world, bluff and hearty. He played bridge and tennis at
the 20-20 Club and took up ballroom dancing. He
made friends with the new rich thrown up by the government's nationalization programmes, made money on
the stock market and moved house to a residential sub-
urb, where he lived in solitary splendour. (His mother
was too ill to move out of her tenement home and died
soon afterwards.) He never saw Suman.

Then, one day, about a year later, he ran across
Nimal at the Galle Face Hotel New Year's Eve dance.
Walter had as usual arrived without a partner, relying
on his charm to avail himself of two semi-detached
ladies and was fetching them and their friends drinks,

when he stumbled against a man on his way to the bar. The man steadied Walter and smilingly offered to help him take the drinks back to his party.

'I am sorry,' gasped Walter, handing him one of the bottles of whisky and a couple of glasses, 'yes, please, thank you. But you must have a drink with us.'

'Later, perhaps,' replied the stranger, excusing himself, and made his way back through the crowd to the other side of the dance floor.

The incident lifted Walter's spirits. Only minutes earlier, he had been complaining to his companions how ill-mannered and inconsiderate people had become since Independence, and here he was, being proved wrong again. 'There's hope for us, yet,' he declared to no one in particular and, picking up his latest attachment, swirled on to the dance floor, to find himself blocked at every turn by drunken stragglers. But he did not mind, his faith in mankind had been restored, the new year would be a new beginning. As midnight struck, he went in search of the attractive stranger with the curly hair and fetching smile who had lit up his evening. People were milling around everywhere, wishing each other a happy new year, and Walter was about to give up the unequal struggle, when someone tapped him from behind and, turning round, he saw the very man he was looking for.

'Happy new year,' they both shouted at the same time and, holding each other up drunkenly, introduced themselves to one another, with neither paying much attention to such mundane details.

'I owe you a drink,' Walter reminded him.

'Have one with me and my wife, first,' said Nimal and led the way to his table. 'This is my wife Kumari and this is —'

'Kumari!'

'Hello, Walter.'

'How lovely to see you,' exclaimed Walter and embraced her. He turned to her husband. 'And you must be Nimal,' and he embraced him. 'What a nice man you are. Congratulations to you both. How's the baby?' he enthused. 'Is it a boy or a girl?'

Nimal and Kumari looked at each other for an answer, and finally Kumari told Walter that there was no baby. She had miscarried, fallen awkwardly during a dress rehearsal, and lost her baby. Broken her ankles too, lost the strength in them, and could no longer go through the rigorous Kathakali sequences.

'Oh God, I've put my foot in it, haven't I? Not foot ... what am I saying? I am so sorry —'

'Don't upset yourself, Walter. You were not to know,' Nimal mollified him. 'Come on, let's drink to the new year. Who knows, it might be an auspicious year for babies.'

Kumari, though, never conceived again, and the growing awareness that she wouldn't brought her and Nimal closer to Walter in a way, united them in a common grief. And Walter was chastened by their company. He still retained his boyish charm and played the reluctant playboy with panache, but he gave up bridge and gambling and his new-rich *mudalali* friends. He preferred to go dancing instead, with Nimal and Kumari, and play tennis with Nimal who, within two years of joining the Club, had become team captain. Walter still carried a torch for Kumari, and it showed, however much he sought alibis in other affairs. (His enemies even put it around that he was still a virgin.)

⁂

That was when I met up with him again, at the height of his performing days. Not that I had not seen it when I was doing my university entrance exams and he was my teacher. Then it was different, flamboyant yes, but restrained, controlled, arising from a consciousness, perhaps, of his duty as a teacher — and he was a grand teacher at that, getting me through to university, despite myself. He was equally subdued with his colleagues in the staff room, and in the school generally, though we had all heard tales of his escapades outside the school walls. Perhaps he had a dual personality — or school may have been too small a stage for him. He needed a motley audience to be at his extrovert best. And the bar at the 20-20 Club invariably promised such a gathering.

I had just returned from England with an MA in Education and, having been appointed Vice-Principal of the Teacher Training College, had approached my old teacher with the offer of a job as Senior Lecturer. But, despite better prospects and a more challenging arena to develop his undoubted talents, he turned the job down. He preferred to work with young people, he said, there was a freshness of hope in them; he was not at ease with the adult world.

We were meeting at the 20-20 Club at the time, and I looked around me with raised eyebrows and commented that there were not many young people there. He laughed and replied, 'That's why I perform.' It was a sudden and unexpected intimacy, and I did not push him to take the job after that. I wanted his friendship more. He seemed to have sensed that, for, having let his mask slip that once, he never put it on again for me – and even when he performed for others, it was not without a sly wink in my direction.

I soon became his closest friend, though I still called him 'Sir', and, little by little, over many evenings of drinking at his club, of which I inevitably became a member, he let fall the story of his love for Kumari. Strangely enough, the telling of the tale seemed to have released him from his pretended love affairs, but he still carried on performing, from memory or from second nature, I could not say.

Five years later, Nimal went down with cancer of the lung. Walter was at his bedside most of the day and all of the night, keeping Kumari's spirits up. Nimal died three weeks later. His last wish was that Kumari should marry Walter.

They were married, appropriately, on New Year's Day 1965. I was the best man. Kumari's mother was too feeble to attend, but Suman was there, greying and handsome. The moment Walter saw him, he engulfed him in his arms, crying, 'Suman, you have come, you have come. Look, Kumari, the professor is here. Did you come for me or for your sister? Oh, it doesn't matter. All that matters is that you have come – after all my neglect of you.' He broke off to introduce me to Suman, but carried on talking to him, asking his forgiveness, afraid of his reproof for the life he had led. I might as well not have been there.

It was a quiet wedding, and the reception a small intimate affair, away from the capital, at the Rest House in Negombo.

I was up very early the next morning, had a run on the beach, and was sitting down to a lonely breakfast, when Kumari walked in dishevelled and in her dressing-gown.

'You knew about this, didn't you?' she asked me wearily, her eyes red with crying.

'Knew what?' I stood up and put out my hand to assuage her distress. 'What's happened?'

'You don't have to pretend. I am getting over it slowly. I had the whole night to get over it. But it was the shock, you see. I never knew, never suspected it for a moment...' She was talking to herself, not to me.

I sat her down gently and let her go on, making sense as best I could.

'Who would have thought it of Walter? But then he didn't know it either, did he?' She looked at me with sad, kindly eyes. 'He didn't come to bed last night. I caught him with Suman.'

I looked at her in dismay.

'Don't be upset,' she chided me. 'He knows now who he is.'

Sri

We killed him, we killed my cousin, Sri: me, his brothers and my father, though he was more father to him than any father Sri could have been born to. We killed him all right, my father mostly. That is all too clear now, but it wasn't then. Certainly, I could not have thought that my father could do wrong. I don't mean intentionally, that he couldn't, no way. I mean sort of inadvertently, without his knowledge, as it were. But then, he was so wise about so many things – he was the guide, the mentor, the father of all our village. Yet it was he who killed Sri. That I know now. How I shall see my father, how I shall focus him, after such knowledge, is another matter.

Sri was a failure, a total, abject failure, everyone in the village said so, or, rather, they said it behind my father's back, beyond Sri's hearing. Sri was an orphan, as were his two brothers. They were my father's children now, he took them all in, all the orphans in the village that is, near relations or far, they were all his responsibility. But Sri and his brothers were his special care: they were the sons of my father's favourite brother who had died young and generous and, inevitably, poor.

Sri's elder brother was a failure too, in a manner of speaking. He kept failing his London Matriculation, but then he was doing it in Colombo, in the metropolis –

and to get to a Colombo school at all was considered an excellence. Sri was stuck in the backwaters of a Jaffna village, five miles from the nearest school, nearest English-teaching school that is. And it was not as though, like his younger brother, he could do well there, either. In fact, his younger brother was a class or two ahead of Sri by the time he was sixteen and well on his way to Colombo and the London Matric.

It was not that Sri did not persevere. He was up at cock-crow every morning and at his books for an hour. After that, he would, unlike his younger brother and his cousins, attend to the cows and the goats and the hens before he left for school. And he was there before them, having walked all five miles of it faster than all the others to get there ten minutes before the bell.

But it was no use. He was the dunce in the class, in every class. They kept him in each for a couple of years and pushed him up thereafter – partly through despair, partly because they could not bear his tortured, appealing face, his squinting eyes and big awkward body in chairs meant for students five years his junior, and partly through a desire to please my father.

By the time Sri was twenty-one and still in the 7th standard, his teachers gave up, and my father gave up, even the school gardener gave up, although Sri was a great help with the jasmines and the oleander and all the other flowers the gardener grew for the school temple.

Sri alone was content. He could tend his cows now, all day long, and his goats and chickens. He could even find time to prune the mango trees and fashion a system of mud-built drains to irrigate the banana plants and the vegetable plots. Not just for himself, but for his neighbours too.

Sri was happy. He woke as usual at five every morning and stayed all the live day long with the animals and trees and all the growing things he loved so much. And the intelligence he brought to them yielded in the village that year a harvest of mangoes and plantains, and brinjals and *bandakka*, and meat and curd and ghee such as it had never, never, known before.

Sri was in his metier. He had a feel for these things; he had found again his rhythm with the world, he was in it, of it, and yet beyond. 'Metier' was a word he gave me the meaning of — not then, watching him, loving him through my boy's eyes, knowing in my boy's tune of soul that he was in time, but later, when I had become mangrown to words in order to find meanings. Yes, it was Sri who gave meaning, content, to 'metier'.

But it wasn't to be for long. The elders of the village were unhappy that my father's nephew should be a cowherd, a peasant, a market-gardener. He had to be in the British civil service somewhere, in the colonial establishment. He had to be there anyway to get married properly, as would warrant a Chief Postmaster's nephew.

So my father, incorruptible man though he was, created, out of that very reputation for incorruptibility, a sub-post office in our village, and a sub-postmastership for Sri.

Six months later Sri was duly married, to his cousin. All was respectability now, the spheres were returned to their orbit, there was balance and peace and heaven.

Except for Sri. Stamps instead of cows, money orders

for goats: the kid that bleated for the udder of its mother now spoke in the staccato terms of a telegram. Sri was lost, confounded, thrown. He had gone sedulously through school, he had married to regulation and had had the regulation kids, he honoured his wife's father and mother, and mine as well — but now ... It was too much for Sri.

A *nalava* woman stood before him, pleading with him to write a letter for her, her sad cow eyes yielding of herself. Sri took her behind the counter, into his arms, against all the rules and fears of caste, offered her betel leaves, suckled at her breast and fed her in the might of his belonging. Sri was free.

In October, a 'shortage' at Sri's sub-post office was reported to the regional head, who, being a friend of my father, informed him straightaway. The old man made good the deficit and admonished Sri not to be extravagant. What on earth was Sri spending his money on?

Three months later, my father made good yet another shortfall, and then again, six weeks after that. Sri's wife and children were almost starving: my father paid for their upkeep. What was Sri doing with his salary?

My father then got his brother, my uncle, a retired station-master, to run things for Sri at the post office. Sri was now sub-postmaster in name only. The village knew it, Sri's friends knew it, but, worst of all, Veena, Sri's untouchable lover, knew it. And she refused to take Sri's money any more, she ceased to be yielding, she no longer came to his hand. One evening, as Sri waited at the palmyra grove, she failed to turn up. That night Sri hanged himself.

The Parolee

Mental Home,
Angoda,
Colombo
2nd August 1983

Dear Raju,

It is over six months since I heard from you. You promised I could come home on parole in May, you promised to send me ten rupees to buy some *bedi*, I have nothing to wear, I sold my sarong to the warder, I must smoke because I cannot eat the food they give me here. You promised to come and see me. You bloody fool why can't you keep your promises? What sort of brother are you? If you go on like this I shan't leave you anything in my will. Ha, ha, I mean the bed bugs and lice and the racing cockroaches I have trained. The fellow in the next bed is quite mad, he says he can tell their form from their colour. I can see no difference, can you?

I am much better now. Soon I shall be well enough to go home for good. I know that it did not work out the last time, but how was I to know a curfew was on? What sort of life is that when a man cannot walk about as he pleases, and twilight is the best time for a walk along the beach, to see the sun go down after its day's work, all red and big and proud. We have no beaches here and no sea to swallow the sun, but at least we can walk where we like. Who wants to go outside anyway, with all these curfews and things.

You shouldn't have slapped me that time. After all I am older than you. I knew you hit me from fear, fear for you and fear for me, fear that the army would shoot me for breaking the curfew. But what is the use of living like that, to other people's orders? One may as well go mad. Ha, ha, I have put one over you there, haven't I?

How is Sister? I did not think she was very happy to see me that last time. Perhaps it was because of those white visitors she had from the High Commission. Well, she should not have told them I was not quite right, just because I spluttered and stuttered over my words and my voice began rising higher and higher. You know how it is when you have been smoking too much, and even without that you know how my thoughts run faster than my tongue and end up by choking me and everybody else? She should not have anyway, because that white man, Green or Brown or some such colour, began talking about me and my mental condition and things as though I was a beetle, and not even a live one at that. Suddenly I saw this beetle on his head, a big one, or perhaps it showed up because he was so bald. And I tried to yell out to him, spluttering of course, tried to warn him that it was going to make a hole in his skull and then he will have to undergo electric treatment like I did — and he just went on talking as though I was the beetle. I wasn't, you know, otherwise I would have poured the soup on myself and not on his head. Oh well, it doesn't matter now. As you know Sister is still very angry about it. She has not even sent me the occasional allowance for smokes and things. Of course, she is silly. With all that education of hers she should know how white men create the monsters that eat them.

Speaking of white men, how is our big brother faring in London? Is he still in that human rights joint, still trying to save white people from themselves, so that they can come and live off us again and send some of us mad? You know I am sure that it is that Viennese specialist, Phoetus or Phoebus or some such fellow who drove me nuts with his bloody electric treatment. Christ, what you people won't do to us to keep us like you.

Who is us anyway? What is so different about you? You are afraid of governments and curfews and things, aren't you? I'm not. Yes, but then I am afraid of thinking. Such thoughts come into my mind, ideas tumbling over each other like the sea, a terrible nightmare picture-show of ideas. It is difficult like now, and so slow, to write like this, but I think a bad period is coming soon, and I won't be able to talk to you at all then.

Yes, when is our London fighter coming? Can't he fight here? Or has the white man got into his brain like the beetle? Really, I think I saved Green that time. Just imagine if I hadn't poured the soup on his head in time. OK, OK, I know I'm laying it on but I don't know any more whether you want me sane or mad and I must admit that I myself find it difficult to work it out at times. Or, perhaps, it's all the time. But I sound all right now, don't I? I know that, you see, I know it

when I am all right, the difficulty is when I am all right
and you all don't know it. I suppose that there are different ways of being all right, but you fellows are in the
majority and won't hear us at all, even when we speak
only for ourselves, unlike you who want to speak for
everybody.

And like our friend over in London, who wants to
look after everybody else but not his own brother. He
can jolly well take a house here in Colombo and take
me to live with him if he was not so all mighty fired
with saving the bloody world. Just save one person?
No, not him.

You know, I think he is quite mad. It was him or
me at one stage. You know that don't you? There he
was, failing all his exams, and falling in and out of love,
and going quietly crazy over a mother he couldn't get
close to – and if I hadn't let him vent his rage and his
frustration on me and beat me up and lock me up in
the woodshed and all those things – if I hadn't let him
do all that, he certainly would have gone mad, and it
would have been him here and not me, and me in
London and not him, except that I know a beetle when
I see one. And after all that I have done for him, he still
... OK it doesn't matter. But tell me, hath any man
greater love than that he saves his brother from mad-
ness by himself going mad?

Yes, yes, I know I write well. Even he, your brother,
the master of the enemy's language, says the same, except that he gets carried away sometimes and says that
if I'm mad, I'm mad like Lear. Lear? I suppose it helps
his conscience to hang his guilt on some learned peg

like that. Hey, that's a good sentence but when it comes like that I know I am already slipping away. But I'll try to hold on, just for a minute more, I must try to hold, hold. There's something I want to say to you, what is it now? You see things are getting dim again so bright they were at the beginning the pictures are rushing past each other the waves the waves ideas tumbling I am drowning my brother my friend but one last thing let me try let me hold one last thing to say.

Now what is it? In this momentary brightness let me. Ah, yes, my mother how is she? Yes my mother not yours or the others', but mine. For you see, though we quarrel like mad – ha, you'll see the sense of that simile in a minute – get on each other's nerves when I'm at home, it is she and she alone who has the feel of me, for she is mad too you know and the only way she can remain that way is to pitch it against my sanity, or vice versa, does it matter? In a way, she will be lost without me, you know. She was not lost without our father. Big man, you think, all loving, all encompassing. Balls. He was a majority man, didn't understand a thing about difference. Yes, yes I know he fought all his life, but like a majority man fights, safely, for somebody, without becoming that other body. OK, OK I am not being quite fair, because he occasionally shades from one to the other. But if I can say that for him why couldn't he say it, why couldn't he see it, for me, as I shaded over? What was he doing there in that bloody shrine room praying to his bloody bloody gods when I wanted him to cradle me in his arms, all sixteen years of me, and give me man-love?

How lucid I have become again. It's not been like this before, Raju, my friend. Something new is happening to me. It's not just pictures and ideas and thoughts that are telescoping inside my head, but all of my life and yours and father's and brother's and *amma*'s, and all so bright and clear and separate, no no never before, not like this, never, I'm afraid Raju, my brother, I'm afraid. I'm afraid I'm going sane.

I made my mother a man to cope with me, our father was in heaven, and even when he was down here, it's the underdog he fought for, not his sons, not me. Is it any wonder that he turned out to be a hypochondriac, all turned inwards — all that outward-bound stuff must have its recompense — hating everybody and loving only himself. Is it any wonder too that my mother, half-blind with cataract, diabetic, irascible and mad, yes mad I tell you, should cope with the world and you and me and bring us up to our full heights.

Don't let me tell you about our younger sister. Let's draw a veil over her, for what else do you do over a cipher?

That's neat, neat I tell you, for with that last sentence I have covered all the family, haven't I? I have made my testament, I mean my statement, the same thing you know, testament, statement, for a mad man, but that he should be lucky to state either? Except yes yes except except it's fading again the clarity it's going the pictures Raju oh God the pictures without a picture just let me hold hold on a minute longer dear bloody bloody gods a minute. You, yes, you, I haven't said anything to you, to you. But it's all right, all right, there's nothing to say. You are a good man, a gentle man and fierce. Thank you, thank you.

There must be a blessing somewhere in the world that it should illumine a mad man's mind before it finally goes dark.

Gunam

Superintendent's Office,
Mental Hospital,
Angoda,
5th August 1983

Dear Sir,

Mr Gunam   D/TL/X24

I regret to inform you that the above passed away last night choking on the bread he was given at supper. His last words were 'Stone I tell you, stone, and don't you dare make that pissing wine into water.'

Of course, he was, as you know, due to go home on a month's parole this weekend, but we expect that he will now spend a well-deserved and prolonged parole in heaven.

I enclose the letter that we found upon his person and await instructions as to the disposal of his remains.

Yours faithfully,
S. L. de Silva
Asst Superintendent

The Homecoming

It had all been arranged: he could go on board the SS *Otranto* when it docked at Southampton to meet his wife and children. He checked the time of arrival yet again with the shipping company. The P&O man was sarcastic; the boat would still be there tomorrow, he said, and the day after and the day after that, and so would his family – no one was going to steal them! The war had been over these last ten years. He laughed at his own joke.

Six more hours to go. How could he while the time away? There was certainly no point in arriving at the dock too early to hang around there with nothing to do. Better tidy up the flat again, rearrange the beds perhaps? Flat? It was no flat, just a large room and kitchenette in the basement of an old Victorian house in Notting Hill – dark and dank, with one window overlooking a wasteland of abandoned machines and broken furniture. But Ravi had brightened the room with flowers and pictures and a bouquet of festive balloons. The two extra lamps he had installed would have made a world of difference, but the landlord had threatened to evict Ravi if he exceeded by so much as a watt the quota of light he was allowed. After all, it was he, the landlord, who paid the bills. That Ravi's rent included a

substantial sum for electric consumption, and that his
rent was itself four times as much as his white neighbours' on the floor above, were not arguments that Mr
Smalec would heed. Ravi could go and find another flat
if he was dissatisfied with this one; nobody was going
to take him in, not with all those brats of his; it was
only because Mr Smalec had once been a refugee himself and had known hardship that he was letting Ravi
and his brood have the flat at all. And, while he was on
the subject, let Ravi remember that the toilet on the
landing above was common to both floors and not
Ravi's personal privy. His kids had better not mess it
up. Did they squat or did they sit? Did they know how
to use toilet paper? He did not want them messing up
the whole place, washing their arses. And mind, lights
out at eleven, and no fiddling with the gas meter.

Five more hours to go. Ravi laid out the towels on
the line over the bath-tub. Well, that at least was something – that they should have a bath in the kitchenette
– no shower like at home, but the rubber contraption
he had bought at Woolworth's would mollify his wife.
The pink towels were for his daughters, Leela and
Shanti, they would like the floral designs on them. For
the little boy, he would be four tomorrow, the towel
with the alphabet and nursery rhyme: he was just beginning to read. And yet more flowers over the cooker for
his wife, they helped to drive the stale smell of cooking
away, better than that horrible chemical stuff he had
been using. He longed, though, for the pungent perfume of jasmine and the queen-of-the-night; the silent
scent of roses and daisies pleased him not as much.

It was time to go. He would collect a couple of magazines at Waterloo and still have time for a coffee before taking the train to Southampton.

The boat had docked by the time Ravi got there, earlier than expected. He was all agog now, anxious to run quickly on board the ship, yearning to hold in his hundred arms his wife and children all at once and for ever, aching to fill that void in him that for six months had cried out daily from a pain of emptiness. But he held himself back, tempering his excitement with reason, letting the others stream out of the boat train, and setting himself down quietly, leisurely, last. As he approached the boat, though, his steps grew quicker. Was it Ram, his son, he saw up there on the deck in the arms of a woman in a sari? He began to run, pushing people aside, frantic to get on board the ship. He was on the top deck now, but his family wasn't there. He ran down a flight of stairs, into the lounge, past the shops, but there was no one there either, none of his countrymen, anyway. He ran towards the purser's office.

'Hey, Ravi, Ravi,' someone called. He turned round; it was Sena.

'Where are they?' he began distraughtly.

'Hey, hey, take it easy man,' admonished his friend, 'they are here all right, upstairs, I just took them up there.'

Ravi leapt up the stairs and literally fell on top of his son who had been keeping watch over that particular staircase.

'*Amma*, *akka*,' Ram yelled to draw his mother's and

sisters' attention, and flung himself into his father's arms.

'*Mahan, mahan,*' the father kept murmuring as he kissed the boy, 'you have grown ... Where are your sisters? Ah *mahal ...*'

He held them all now in his manifold arms, the old pain lifting, but the filling of the void was unbearable too; so long had he been empty that to be filled again so suddenly and so fully was a pain beyond all bearing. He set his son down and embraced, alone, his wife. 'My life,' he whispered, the man who had died.

∾

'I will pay the taxi off, you go on and open the door,' he instructed his wife. 'Go on, here's the key. Leela and Shanti, get hold of Ram, he's running down the road.'

His wife stood still, irresolute against the grey of the building. But the children, happy in their father and the July sun, pushed their mother towards the door. Ravi took the key from his wife, ushered them in, along the corridor, down the steps, to the door of their own little room.

'It's so dark suddenly,' said Leela darting into the room. 'There is no sunshine here. Stop playing with those light switches, Shanti,' she scolded her sister. 'Ram, where's Ram, hiding again are you? Come on, *appa* is calling.'

'I wrote to you about the flat, didn't I,' Ravi held out to his wife tentatively at the door. 'So you won't be surprised that you've got to go through the kitchen to come to the sitting-room?'

'Nothing matters,' she replied, taking his hand in

hers, 'nothing matters; we are together, that's enough.'

'The kitchen is not bad,' she added, going through it to the bedroom. 'Where's the sitting ... Oh, it's all one, is it? But you have arranged it all beautifully, Ravi, the children's beds in that corner, ours here in this, and the table and chairs in the centre – that's fine, it's lovely, better than I expected from what you said in your letters. And the flowers...'

'*Appa*,' cried Ram, 'where is the sun? Why are there no windows? Can I climb the mango tree? What is this lamp, it gives a horrible smell, I feel sick.'

'That's not a lamp, son,' said Ravi softly, 'that's a heater, a paraffin heater, we need it in this country, to keep warm, even in the summer. There are no trees here. I'll take you after lunch to see some in the park.'

'They are not like our flowers are they?' asked Shanti, pulling the petals off the roses, as Leela came rushing back from the kitchen.

'*Appa*, I can't find the lavatory, where is it? And please, *appa*, can I have a shower?'

Ravi looked at his children, trying to answer them all at once, and suddenly he knew he had no answers. He had taken them out of the green and the sun and the trees and the sea-air of their country, out of the warmth and friendship and love of all the homes once so open around them, to a bleak land of grey-grief summers far from the swell of the sea, with a place for flowers and a place for trees, and no place for children, and a house among houses that yielded no home. He wept.

The Man Who Loved the Dialectic

There was no one at his graveside except me, the publican from the Horse and Hound and a small dark woman dressed in black, whom I took to be Clarence's sister. I couldn't be sure, though, because Clarence never spoke about the members of his family other than his father, whom he loathed and loved in equal measure. All I knew was that he had a sister living in London somewhere.

'You are not Clarence's sister, by any chance, are you?' I asked, going up to the figure in black. She looked up from beneath her broad-brimmed hat, took one look at me and shuffled off on short, stumpy legs. There was no mistaking that walk: she was Clarence's sister all right.

I went after her and caught up with her at the bus-stop.

'Please,' I said. 'I am Bala, Clarence's friend.'

She looked me up and down from a height of four foot eleven, and I winced.

'Friend, ha?' she said at last. 'So what do you know about me? Friend?'

'Nothing, er ... how do you mean?'

'Clarence never told you anything about me, did he?'

'No, he didn't, but I knew —'

'That I existed. Yes, that's about all he knew too.' She broke off as a No 34 bus hove into view, but she did not attempt to get on it. Instead, she went and sat on a bench in the shelter, emptied now of all but her and me. 'Yes, that's about all he knew,' she repeated, gazing into the distance.

'I don't understand . . .'

'He was ashamed of me, you see.' She took out a handkerchief from her handbag and blew her nose.

'Ashamed? Surely not?' I remonstrated weakly.

'Because I had no proper education and I only came to England as a nanny to the Ceylon High Commissioner . . . to be near him . . . he was our hope . . . but he, he . . .' She began to cry and I sat down by her side and put a tentative arm around her.

'I saw him once or twice in the beginning when he used to come for his rice and curry to the High Commission canteen, but then my boss got transferred and I went to work at Woolworth's in Croydon.'

I still could not quite understand why Clarence, who only had a clerical job himself, would look down on her.

'Maybe he didn't have the time,' she smiled, and the years lifted from her face. 'What with all that writing he was doing, and the distance. Do you live in Hampstead too?'

'Hampstead? Er, no. What writing?'

'You know, all that political —'

'Ah, that,' I dissembled. Clarence to my knowledge had never written anything in his life.

'You probably know him better than I do,' and she rose to go as another 34 came along. 'I'll have to take this bus or I'll be late, but please come and see me.' She scribbled her number on my newspaper, 'And tell me all about him. Next Sunday?'

'Yes, fine.'

'Bye, Bala.'

'Bye...'

'Betty.'

'Bye, Betty.'

☙

I had not known Clarence that well. There was something about him that had made me keep my distance. Yet, I had gone to his funeral. I had gone to pay my respects to a dead man whom, alive, I did not respect at all. Normally, I wouldn't have given the matter another thought, but my conversation with Betty left me feeling that I might have been as ashamed of him as he was of her.

I first met Clarence over a game of billiards at the YMCA in Colombo. I had just got through my degree and been called for an interview at the Bank of Ceylon that morning. And, as I was a nervous hour too early, I had strayed into the YMCA next door for a cup of tea and a calming game of billiards. The billiard room was empty – it was still too early for the *habitués* – except for this one solitary figure who, from the grunts of victory that emanated from him, seemed to enjoy playing against himself.

'Would you mind if I –' I began.

'Not at all,' he broke in. 'I was waiting for someone

to beat other than myself. My name is Clarence.'

'Bala,' I said, and offered him my hand.

'Half an hour? Five rupees?'

'Fine,' I replied and, taking off my jacket, laid it carefully on one of the high seats that ranged the walls.

'Going somewhere?' he asked, chalking his cue.

'Interview. Next door.'

'Oh? Clerk?'

'No. Staff officer.'

'Oh-h,' this time he dragged out the oh. 'Staff officer, hah? So you are a graduate?'

I nodded.

'I am a graduate, too,' he laughed, and added, 'from the university of life.'

Whatever university he was from, I was certainly no match for him at this game. I had opened the frame nonchalantly and left him with a difficult in-off. But from that slender chance, he had already built up a break of 53. As he reached across the table to put the red into the far corner, I noticed how elongated his body was from the waist up. His legs were short and fat and barely reached the ground, and his face was as long and lean and ugly as his torso. A body built for billiards, I thought ruefully, as I saw my lunch money disappear.

'Here, let me buy you a cup of tea,' he said when the game was over. 'Have you got time?'

'Just about,' I replied, and accompanied him to the restaurant.

He bought me tea, but I had to pay for the biscuits. Was he mean or not very well off? He was dressed neatly but not expensively in a long-sleeved cotton shirt and white satin-drill trousers.

'Where do you work?' I asked.

'At the Lake House bookshop, but I took the day off to catch up with my reading,' and, seeing my quizzical look, he went on, 'here at the YMCA library.'

'Ah.'

'I am just marking time, you see – before I go to England.'

I was curious to know what he was going to England for, but I was getting late for my interview. So I bade him good luck and left.

॰

Strangely enough, the next time I saw him was in London, some five years later. I had gone to Compendium to pick up some books that I had ordered from America when I felt a tap on my shoulder and, turning round, saw a short dark man in a pipe and Harris tweed jacket smiling at me from under his glasses. I could not place him at first, but his voice, as he said, 'Bala, isn't it?' sounded familiar.

'Ye-es. You are?'

'Clarence. Remember? The YMCA? Colombo?'

'Oh my God, yes. It was ages ago. Clarence. You beat me at billiards.'

'And you were going for an interview. What happened? Hey, you are not the manager of the Bank of Ceylon, London branch, are you?'

'No, no, nothing like that. Thanks to you, I was late for the interview and I didn't get the job.'

'Oh, I say. I am sorry.' He looked genuinely upset

46

and I quickly reassured him that I was only joking, and it had all turned out for the best anyway. I was not fitted to be a banker.

'I tried to tell the Chairman of the Interview Board that if I was three minutes late, it was because I had been an hour too early – and had therefore gone for tea. And you know what that pompous ass said,' and here I tried to imitate old Farquhar's public school accent. '"Logic and punctuality are the cardinal virtues of banking. You lack both. Good day."'

Clarence burst out laughing and his mournful face looked pleasing for a moment. 'So, what are you doing now?'

'I am lecturing at Peradeniya. Came over a couple of months ago to do a PhD at the LSE. And you?'

'Oh, I thought I'd come over and see what the mother country was like, you know. That was four years ago and I am none the wiser.' He sucked at his unlit pipe. 'And I do a bit of freelance writing for the Lake House papers back home.'

'You are a journalist now?'

'Something like that, but I do a job in the local council as well. Keep the home fires burning, eh?' and he chuckled uneasily. 'Look, I have to go, but ring me, here's my number and we'll have a drink some time.'

I never got round to ringing Clarence. He was only a casual acquaintance, after all, and he had probably given me his number by way of welcoming a newcomer. Then, one day, a couple of months later, I got a call from him. I did not know where he got my number from. I was living in Harrow with my sister at the time and had no wish to invite him over. But he saved me the embarrassment by asking me to join him and his friends in a drink at his local pub on his birthday.

'Do you know the Horse and Hound in Hampstead?' he asked. 'Seven o'clock then. Friday.'

I did not know why Clarence had asked me, but I was even more nonplussed when I got to the pub to discover that he had invited only a few close friends, and they all knew each other. I was the outsider. But, as the evening wore on and the conversation turned to the sit-ins at the universities, I got the impression that they all belonged to some sort of Marxist study-group, and I had been brought in to give the low-down on the LSE. Or, that is what I gathered from the way Clarence introduced me to his friends.

'This is the bloke I told you about. Bala. He knows everything that is going on at the LSE.' I opened my mouth to protest, but Clarence held up an imperious hand. 'There's no need for modesty among comrades,' he said, and I realized that I had to play along: I was his contribution to their discussion on student politics, the missing ingredient in their theoretical formulations, the view from the ground, the voice from the barricades. Only, I was not sure how to play my role: as a red insurrectionary or as a black militant – since the rest of them, four men and two women, were all white, and Clarence, up to now, must have provided 'the coloured perspective'. But the questions they fired at me were to do with the goings-on at the college, and I managed to skirt them without betraying my ignorance. They, however, put it down to a commendable caginess on my part and bought me another drink on the strength of it.

Only when the conversation drifted towards the events in the United States and the civil rights movement did I have to put on my black hat. On that subject, though, I managed to be quite informative – since it formed the major part of my dissertation – and, on the basis of that, made myself eligible for another free drink or two. But Tessa, the fairer of the two women, kept bringing the discussion back to England and what coloured people here should do about the immigration laws, now that Labour had adopted them too. I had no answer to that one, and I looked to Clarence as the senior immigrant to provide it, but he mumbled and spluttered incoherently about the responsibility of the mother country to its children and ended up declaring 'we are here because you were there'. I was sure that I had heard that slogan before, from the lips of an anti-colonial ranter at Speakers' Corner perhaps, and I doubted that Clarence understood its full import, but the others thought how original and brilliant he was. And Tessa, who was seated next to him, put her arms round him and kissed him.

I left shortly afterwards, but not before I had been persuaded to participate in one of their study-group sessions the following Saturday. It was all very informal, they assured me, and Tessa, in whose flat it was being held, would be cooking rice and curry, Tamil style.

I was wary about attending the Marxist class, the subject of discussion being 'The Eighteenth Brumaire of Louis Bonaparte', about which I knew nothing. But I wanted to see Tessa again. She was not pretty in the conventional sense, and her tall, trim figure was eloquent without being evocative, but there was a luminosity about her face that went with the enthusiasm with which she embraced everyone around her. She couldn't have thought ill of anyone even if she tried, least of all Clarence, for whom she seemed to have a special affection. I could not let that put me off though and, hoping to see her alone, I arrived at her house off Haverstock Hill long before the others.

'Oh, it's you, Bala,' she said, opening the door to me.

'Am I too early?'

'A bit, yes, but that doesn't matter. It gives us a chance to get to know each other better.'

'I brought you these.' I held out a bunch of roses.

'For me? But no one these days ... Oh all right. Thanks.' She took my coat and hung it up on a rack under the staircase.

'I am just putting the finishing touches to my curry,' she announced, leading the way into the kitchen. As I followed her down the hall, I noticed that her hair, which had been bunched up in a becoming black beret when I saw her in the pub, now fell in ripples to her shoulders. And her walk was light and graceful.

'Try this,' she said, offering me a piece of curried chicken.

'H'mm. Good. What's that simmering? It's not −'

'Yes, *rasam*. What us English mistakenly call mulligatawny.'

'May I?' I took a ladle full and put it to my mouth.

'Brilliant. Absolutely brilliant. Just the right amount of tamarind. That's the most difficult thing to get right, you know, *rasam*. You're sure you are not a Tamil?'

She threw her head back and laughed. I liked her laugh, I liked her throat, I liked . . . I caught myself.

'Who taught you?' I inquired.

'Clarence. It was he who got me the recipe anyway. I can't do without it now.' She made a face as though to apologize for her self-indulgence. 'But really, no rice meal is complete without it, is it?'

'Certainly not a Tamil one. It's supposed to be an antidote to the hot curries we eat, settles the stomach.'

She finished her cooking and we took our glasses into the sitting-room. Bob Dylan was singing 'Maggie's Farm' in the background.

'Have you known him long?'

'Who? Clarence? Long, yes, but well, no.' She smiled and I liked her mouth, though I had not liked thin lips on women before; they suited her, went with her long, pale Modigliani face. 'He hasn't had much of a life, has he? But he won't talk about it to me.'

I told her that I had not known Clarence that long – I had met him only a couple of times before – and tried to steer the subject round to her, but without much success. All I could gather was that her father was a banker of sorts and the house belonged to him. She was there, temporarily, till she got her own place, had been looking for two years now but could find nothing she could afford, not on her pay, anyway, as an editorial assistant at Penguin's.

'But this place is too big for one person when there

are so many homeless. Look at it ... lounge, dining-room, study, four bedrooms, two baths. I told Clarence ... oh yes, but no washing machine,' she broke off, smil-ing at some private joke. 'Otherwise I'd never have met him,' she chuckled. 'I told Clarence he could come and live here, he is here most of the time anyway, but he wouldn't move out of his damn bed-sitter. On princi-ple!' She threw up her eyes to heaven. Hers were bluer.

'Perhaps he likes to stick to one –'

'Oh no, he moves all right, but from one bed-sitter to another every time the landlord puts the rent up. The whole of that area around the square where he lives is bed-sitter land. That's how those bastards make their money, renting out horrible little rooms with gas ring and heater-with-meter to coloured immigrants. Do you know how much Clarence pays?' The conversation went back to Clarence, and I gave in reluctantly, want-ing to know more about their relationship and afraid that I'd find out.

They had met in a launderette some four years ago. He was still new to the country, he had told her, (although on my calculations he had arrived a year earlier, in 1963) and did not know how to work the washing machine. She was the only other person in the launderette – it was early morning of a stone-grey autumn Sunday – and she helped him out. He was at the launderette again the following Sunday and they had struck up an acquaintance. It was still cold and grey and he invited her to his 'humble abode' for a cup of hot coffee and, before she could even reply, had declared that he would understand if she refused. She couldn't turn him down after that.

'I can't refuse him anything really,' she confessed, pouring more wine into my glass. 'Not that he asks for much,' and she went on to describe how simply he lived, like a true socialist. '"We must subtract, not add", he says.' I looked quizzically at her — the line rang a bell, from a film somewhere, Renoir perhaps — but she thought I had not understood, and was keen to explain. 'Subtract from our wants, that is, not add to our needs.'

'Ah-hah.'

'He was very angry when he first came to my place and saw how well off I was.' She was standing by the French windows, glass in hand, long and lissom in her kaftan against the watery light of a spring evening, and I could not help thinking in how many different ways I could love her. 'I pointed out to him that it was my father's house and not mine, that it was the system he should be angry with, not the individual.' She drew the curtains and put the lights on, lighting up a Lowry over the fireplace. 'So much anger he had, God, and didn't know how to channel it. So I got him to join our study-group.'

'Are you in love with him?' I blurted out.

'You are very blunt,' she said, resuming her seat and lighting a cigarette.

'That's because you are so open.' The colour rose all the way from her neck to her high-boned cheeks. 'Are you? In love with him?'

'No-oo. I don't think so. Maybe. From time to time.

Oh, I don't know, Bala.' (She lingered over the Ba.) 'Besides, he has so many women friends. In fact, he rang just before you came to ask whether he could bring someone called Stella for dinner.' She shrugged her shoulders. 'I hadn't even heard of her. He only dropped the idea when I reminded him about the class.'

There was a chance here for me, I thought, and was about to ask her out to the theatre when the door opened and a whole lot of Tessa's friends poured noisily in.

'The front door was open,' apologized Tom, whom I had met in the pub and took to be the leader of the group. He was a sociology lecturer at the Kilburn Polytechnic.

'Yes, I know,' replied Tessa, and introduced me to a couple of people I had not met before.

A little while later, Clarence appeared, in his customary tweed jacket and pipe, *The Communist Manifesto* peering out of his pocket.

'Are we all here, then?' asked Tom, counting out the seven seated in a circle on the floor. I quickly got off my chair and joined them.

'Where's Barbara?'

'She rang to say she couldn't get a baby-sitter and might be late,' Tessa informed him.

Tom looked at his watch. 'It's past six and we've probably got an hour and a half before dinner. Tessa?' She nodded. 'Let's begin then. Trevor,' he turned to a sallow young man in a limp roll-neck jumper seated next to him. 'Your turn to lead off the discussion.'

Trevor cleared his throat and threw up his head. 'Men make their own history but they do not make it just as they please,' he declaimed, and for a moment I thought they were his lines, so changed was he by their mere utterance. The shyness was gone, there was colour in his cheeks and even his jumper seemed to have sprung back to life. 'What I think Marx was trying to say there,' he went on authoritatively, but I was so taken up with his transformation that I lost the thread of his argument. I took to watching the others, instead, to see how they were reacting – to find that they were equally earnest, some even taking notes. Except for Clarence and a little round girl in a little round dress and little round shoes whom everybody knew as Slim. Clarence dragged on his pipe and took little part in the discussion except to snort in anger or disgust from time to time, and Slim dozed off, awoke, smiled, and dozed off again. When it came to my turn to make a contribution, I echoed something Tessa had said (about what I can no longer remember) and they all politely nodded.

My small talk over dinner, though, put the group at ease with me and I was generally accepted as a fellow traveller. Clarence, taking it as a compliment to him, insisted that I should come to his 'digs' for a meal.

'I would like that,' I said, hoping to put him off, but he took out his diary and arranged to have me over for dinner on the last Sunday of the month.

I waited till everybody had gone to have a private word with Tessa, but Clarence was clearly staying the night and I left with a heavy heart. I rang her a few times after that, but got no reply – and I anxiously counted the days to Clarence's dinner when I'd see her again.

But when that day finally arrived, there was no Tess. Instead, there was Stella, Clarence's recent acquisition, comely and comfortable, so unlike Tessa, who was lively and challenging. The disappointment must have shown in my face because Clarence took me to one side and whispered that he had something for me too.

'What do you mean?' I asked but, before he could reply, there was a knock on the door and a bubbly young woman floated in.

'Bala, this is Esther. Esther, Bala.' Clarence smiled benignly. 'Why don't you open the bottle of wine you brought, Bala? The glasses are in the kitchen.'

The kitchen turned out to be an alcove tucked away at the end of the L-shaped bed-sitting room. It consisted of a small table, a wall-cupboard, a vegetable rack under the sink and a two-burner stove. But on this, I discovered, when driven by curiosity to take a peek into the pans on the table, Clarence had managed to turn out a goodly meal for four – with mutton curry, fried bitter gourd, dhal and yellow rice. I was just tasting the curry when Clarence walked in.

'Nice, hah? The way to a woman's you-know-what is through the stomach,' he cackled, rummaging in the drawer for a corkscrew.

'Tessa's too?' I could not help asking.

'No, in her case it's through the head.' He took a couple of glasses off me. 'Come on, let's drink.'

Clarence was an attentive host and the girls cheerful

company, but the conversation was all about overtime and tea-breaks and how much better local government was — Stella and Esther both worked in the DES, and Clarence in Camden Council — and I had nothing to say. Esther, who was doing evening classes in Current Affairs, made an effort to draw me into the conversation by inquiring about the 'happenings' at the LSE. I was beginning to make a pretty good case for student rebellion when Clarence stepped in and declared that only workers like Stella and Esther and himself could bring out real changes in society, make a revolution, in fact. For, what is a revolution, he asked weightily, and then went on to address the question himself in vague Marxian phrases that the girls clearly admired and I could hardly follow. But I cornered him in the kitchen as he went to fetch more drinks.

'What was that all about?' I asked.

'How the hell should I know?' he replied indifferently, and offered me a choice of wine, beer or whisky. 'Ask the girls what they'll have.'

Neither Stella nor Esther wanted a drink. They preferred to eat instead, and so did I. Clarence, though, insisted on feeding us before he sat down to his meal.

'Why doesn't he eat with us?' inquired Esther of Stella, when Clarence had gone to the kitchen.

'Oh, he's always doing that. Is it a custom?' Stella turned to me.

'Not that I know of.'

Clarence returned with a pan in one hand and a ladle in the other.

'More mutton, gravy, anyone?' he asked holding the

pan over our plates in succession.

'Yes, please,' said Stella. 'Here, Clarence, Esther wants to know why you don't eat with us?'

'Habit, I suppose.' He put down the pan and picked up his glass of whisky. 'My mother never ate till all of us were fed. There was not enough to go round sometimes, and sometimes she had nothing.' He drained his glass and poured himself another. 'But I didn't know that till I was much older, none of us did, except my father, perhaps, though he ate in the church most times; people brought him food, he was the sacristan.'

Clarence was talking to himself more than to us, and he was drinking steadily.

'You must eat,' Stella urged him, collecting the empty plates. 'Shall I serve you?'

'You can't let all that nice food go to waste,' said Esther.

But Clarence was too far gone into himself to hear them.

'Why?' he muttered.

'What?' Stella had just come back into the room. 'What did you say?' She sat beside him on the sofa.

'My folk are starving while I...' He spoke hardly above a whisper and I could barely make out the words, but the girls, seated on either side of him, flung their arms around him as though to save him from some natural disaster. And I was beginning to think that Clarence had worked getting sympathy to a fine art when he suddenly leapt from the sofa, shouting, 'Bastards, bastards, they are all bastards,' and angrily paced the room.

'Who?' I was surprised into asking.

'The Portuguese, the Dutch, the British. All those buggers who stole our country from us and left us with these.' He pointed to his trousers and shoes. 'And this.' He pulled at the cross that hung on a chain around his neck.

His anger threw me and, for a moment, I could not get my words out. 'But they also gave us railways and roads and an English education,' I heard myself say, as from a distance. And hadn't Marx himself said that capitalism was good for us?

That only sent Clarence into another paroxysm of rage. 'Bugger Marx,' he yelled. 'What the hell did he know about us?' He stopped in mid-stride and went back to his drink. 'Did he know my father?' he whispered, peering into his glass, 'and how he sold out his faith to send me to a Christian school, for your bloody English education?' His voice rose in anguish again, but this time it was his eloquence that took me aback. Usually when he was angry, he choked on his words or stuttered and snorted, his anger spoke in his face. Now, suddenly, it had broken its barrier and burst into speech.

But, as suddenly as it had erupted, it died – and landed him on a bean-bag on the floor. He struggled out of it into a sitting position, muttering an apology.

'I am sorry. I don't know what came over me.' He smiled, trying to put his face back on, but sank back into the cushion, holding his head in his hands. 'I don't understand anything any more. I don't understand me. I don't understand the world ... My brain is bursting.'

He shook his head from side to side, and something stirred deep down in my memory. I had been there, too, with those questions, a long, long time ago, before I went to university. And for a moment I felt sorry for Clarence. He had not been as lucky as me.

I saw Clarence a few times after that at demonstrations and meetings, with Tessa mostly, but I was still suffering the pangs of unrequited love to accept their invitations to dinner. I did go to one more of their weekly study-group sessions, though, some six months later, to find that the subject of discussion had moved on from Marx's political writings to his more philosophical outpourings, and I did not stay very long. Clarence, on that occasion, looked more drawn and haggard than usual, and a little the worse for drink, but I did not give the matter much thought. Till I heard from Stella a few days later that Clarence had taken his life. Only then did it occur to me that he had the same haunted look at the meeting that he had had when I left his place after dinner that night, all those months ago.

I ran over Stella's account in my mind again as I went to see Betty a week after the funeral, but I was undecided whether to acquaint her with the full circumstances of her brother's death. As far as I could tell, she thought that Clarence had been knocked down by a van as he was reeling drunkenly across the road from the Horse and Hound shouting something unintelligible — or that was what the police had told her. According to Stella, however, Clarence had been drinking heavily for some time, and his bouts of anger had become so manic that he had lost most of his friends.

He had often, in his cups, mumbled to her some non-sense about looking for his life, but she had paid him little mind. But on that last drink-sodden evening with her, which happened to be the day before I last saw him, he had suddenly declared that if he could not find his life, he might as well end it.

'Are you sure you heard him right?' I asked Stella.

'Oh, yes. Those were his very words. If I can't find my life, Stella, I may as well end it. No question. You know how he usually blathers on and you don't know what the hell he is talking about, and then he has these flashes of ... I don't know what, and you are so shocked, you listen to every word?' She paused and I heard her transfer the phone to her other hand. 'I listened all right and those were his very words, I tell you.'

I was afraid that Stella was right, but Betty, I realized the moment I saw her, had already come to terms with her brother's death, and I did not want to say anything that would upset her. She had just returned from church when she opened the door to me and still had her veil and missal in her hand.

'Is this a bad time...' I began tentatively, remembering how acerbic she could be.

'No, no, it's a good time. I have just been putting Clarence to rest — in my mind.'

She led me into the tiny sitting-room and went off to make a pot of tea.

'How is it that there were no friends of Clarence's at the funeral?' she called out, and I trotted out some excuse about people being on holiday at this time of year (Tessa certainly was) and that, in any case, the death was sudden and the funeral unannounced. (Stella had had to go to Glasgow for her brother's wedding.)

The flat was small and tidy and bare of comfort. There were two photographs on the sideboard, one of an old man whom I took to be her father, and another of Clarence, in hat and overcoat, taken in a park somewhere in London. There was none of her.

'Do you live alone?' I asked Betty when she came back with the tea.

'No, I am not married, if that's what you are getting at,' she laughed, putting me at my ease.

'Was Clarence the only family you had, then? In London I mean?'

'Yes. I have five sisters back home, and my father is still alive. Mother died giving birth to Edna, my last sister. Clarence was the only boy and the eldest. I was next. Six girls and one boy, and we all looked up to him.' She got up to offer me a biscuit and I noticed how much she looked like Clarence, except that her prematurely greying hair gave a more agreeable cast to her face.

'It will kill the old man, you know, Clarence's death. He has heart trouble and is partially blind ... and he was waiting for the day his son would come back and make up with him.'

'Make up?'

'Yes. Clarence and father never got on. They loved each other, but they never got on. Something happened to Clarence, you see, when father converted to Catholicism. He was only five years old at the time, but he was already a good Hindu boy, going to temple with father and mother and singing *thevarams*, he had such a lovely voice – and he used to ring the bell for the priest.' She trailed off into reminiscences of her brother, like a vast release, and I did not like to interrupt her. But from what I managed to piece together, it was clear that Clarence had never quite forgiven his father for selling out his faith. He had understood as he grew older that the only way his father, a lowly clerk, could pay for his son's education at the local mission school was with the price of his faith, but Clarence was never able to reconcile himself to it entirely. The way Betty told it, there had always been in Clarence a dumb anger at his father's sacrifice. It was as though he felt the pain of his father's self-betrayal more keenly than the old man himself – and there was nothing he could do about it.

Or that is how the story came across to me when I had managed to unravel Betty's painful recollections. And I went home a troubled man – so much of Clarence's life touched on mine and I was beginning to feel uncomfortable with myself. Besides, I had come to like Betty and felt bad that I had not told her the truth about Clarence's death.

The next evening I had a call from Tessa. She had just returned from Cuba and heard that Clarence had committed suicide. I tried to comfort her, but she was inconsolable, and I hired a taxi and went over to see her.

But when I got there, she was laughing through her tears and greeted me with shouts of 'It was an accident,

an accident. He never took his life. He never would.'
With that, she dragged me by the hand into the sitting-
room and handed me a letter.

'Clarence's,' she said. 'I only found it after I rang
you.' She took the letter back from me. 'But before you
read it, let me explain that it was written after that last
class you came to. Remember? On dialectical material-
ism? Clarence got thoroughly excited about it. But you
had left by then.' She put the letter back in my hand.
'You can read it now.'

*Tess, my love. It's the dialectic. It just struck me as I
got home. Everything is the dialectic. Don't you see? All
that other stuff we have been reading is rubbish without
the dialectic. Only the dialectic matters. It explains
everything – my father, my country, me. At last, at last,
I understand. Everything is contradiction, conflict, life
grows out of conflict, life is zig-zag, not a straight line.
Nothing is finished, everything is beginning.*

*At last I have something which does not separate
what I know from what I have been taught. I have
light, I have God, I have my Tess.*

Ah, the dialectic. I love the dialectic.

*P.S. I am going to the Horse and Hound for my last
booze-up to celebrate the dialectic. See you, sober, after
you get back.*

The Car

The brakes still squeaked. Mano had botched up the
job, for the second time. Of course, the car was over six
years old, a '59 Ford Anglia with God knows how
many thousand miles on the clock. But that was no excuse really. The least he could do was to ring Mano and
give him a piece of his mind: he had already paid him
£20 just to get the brakes done. True, Mano had tried
to keep the expenses as low as possible, he was not the
boss, after all; the garage belonged to his uncle. Even
so, he might have done a better job of it. And the more
Deva found explanations for Mano, the more it made
him angry.

'Mano,' he began aggressively, 'this is Deva here.
Those damn brakes you did for me last week. Did you
really do them or –'

'What *machan*,' interrupted Mano, using a term of
endearment which literally meant brother-in-law but
implied that you were one's kin by choice. 'You don't
believe that I –'

'No, no, I didn't mean that, I am sorry,' retreated
Deva, shamed out of his suspicion. 'You know that I
know very little about cars. It was simply that ... You
see the brakes are still pretty squeaky. In fact, the noise
is worse than before.'

'Yeah, yeah. I'll tell you what. Leave the car with me this weekend. Till Monday evening? I can then look into all the other little defects which you wanted me to look at too. I can take the car to technical college, do it there, can't do much in the garage with my uncle looking on, it will be too expensive. How about that? Can you manage without the car for a couple of days?'

By now, Deva was thoroughly ashamed of himself. In his embarrassment he turned from aggressor to supplicant, yielded to Mano's knowledge of cars and rendered himself ignorant.

'It is all right, is it, to run the car like that? It won't damage ... I mean it is not against the law or something?'

'No, no,' Mano laughed. 'Of course it isn't. And there is no harm to the car, probably some dirt in the brake drums. Bring it in, we will see, and if you are still so keen to sell it, I'll try and find a buyer for you.'

'Yes, Mano, let's do that. I have had the car for ages and I'd like a change. But even if you sell mine, say for £150, what can I get for a couple of hundred quid? That's all I can manage.'

'I say, *machan*, there's a good Peugeot that's going cheap. The owner, a French woman, is going back home. She'll take a hundred pounds, if it's a quick sale.'

'Can't be very good, then,' said Deva.

'Oh no, they are damned good engines. Peugeots never die,' he laughed. 'I'll sort something out for you. Don't worry.'

'OK, Mano, see you Saturday.'

On Monday evening, when Deva went to pick up the car, nothing had been done.

'I say, *machan*, I am sorry. My lecturer didn't turn up and I couldn't take the car into the workshop. I'll tell you what, bring it on Friday, no Thursday, and leave it for two days with me. I need two days at least; there is a lot to be done on the car. OK?'

'Yes, OK,' said Deva sceptically. He was not sure how much of Mano's story was true. But he had no choice but to go along with the other's plans. It was too late to back out without hurting Mano's feelings. Besides, he might be telling the truth: that he hadn't been able to do it over the weekend but would do it soon. It was up to Deva to interpret it – to accept Mano's explanation literally or metaphorically, without being certain of either. The truth or otherwise of Mano's statement was not important. What mattered was the goodwill, the intention, the affection it demonstrated.

'What about the Peugeot?' Deva asked.

'Ah yes, the Peugeot. Mark has seen it, thinks it's damned good value. But let me have a look at it too before I commit you.'

'OK, Mano. Thanks. I'll leave the car with you on Thursday, and come for it on the Saturday after?'

On Friday afternoon, Deva received a call from Mano.

'*Machan*,' he began. 'I have got a buyer for your car. £125. That's good. He is coming to see it this evening. What do you say?'

'Yes Mano, by all means sell it, if you think the price is right.'

'And I'll go and see the Peugeot, too, later this evening. OK?'

'Yes, fine. But won't you require my registration card and things to do the deal? Do you want me to bring them over?'

'No, that won't be necessary at this stage. I'll get a deposit off the buyer, if the price is right.'

'What about the repairs then? I mean if he doesn't want to buy. Can I pick up the car tomorrow? Is everything done?'

'Well, I haven't done any major repairs. No point, if we are going to sell it. But everything else is OK. I'll give you a ring. Or, better still, come into the garage tomorrow.'

Deva was apprehensive. All that Mano had said might be true. There might indeed be a buyer for his car, and if he himself bought the Peugeot, he would still be £25 to the good. And, of course, there was no point in undertaking major repairs if the car was going to be sold. On the other hand, it was likely that Mano was stalling for time to complete the job on his car. But then, why the story about the Peugeot? A little embellishment perhaps, typical of his countrymen: people ran away with their stories. Not likely, though. Mano wouldn't complicate matters for himself. The relationship was already getting thin. If he went too far out on a limb, it would be difficult to climb down. If both deals fell through, Mano would have one hell of a time matching his stories without conveying, at the same time, his loss of good intentions, of affection. The car thing, after all, was not important, the friendship was.

'*Machan*,' Mano said as Deva went up to him in the garage on Saturday, 'the car is ready. It's all done, not the major repairs of course...'

'But what happened to the —'

'Ah yes. Hell of a thing, no, man. That fellow who wanted to buy your car? He bought the Peugeot.'

The Playwright and the Player

I met them quite by chance. Exhibitions usually bored me, especially when they tried to capture 2,000 years of a culture as rich as India's within the four walls of a grey Victorian building. But I had accompanied Nancy that morning to her interview at the Greater London Council and had drifted towards the Tate whilst waiting for her.

The gallery was full of people, mostly tourists, and, judging from their charmless manners and their astonished cries at sighting civilization, mostly American. Only in the middle of the hall, but some way to the left, did there appear to be any breathing space, and I hurried quickly past the artefacts of the Harappan civilization and the photomontages of Mohenjodaro to the vacant seat ahead of me – and suddenly I realized why there were so few people there. For, before me, set in a stone tablet that spanned the wall, were the sculpted figures of the Khajuraho lovers, fucking all heaven into each other. It was not a sight for genteel eyes, and the visitors passed it in self-conscious haste. Occasionally, a little boy or girl would stop to giggle and be hauled away disgustedly by a righteous parent. Only these two remained beside me, this man and woman enwrapped in each other, and themselves turned to stone, as they watched the Gods make love on a temple wall in ancient India.

I had not noticed the couple at first: I was gone into the stone myself, with my own thousand loves and longings, caught up in the exquisite anguish of its unfulfilled ecstasy. I had been aware that they were there in my moments of consciousness but, even then, it was the woman I had seen and not the man — and not seen so much as sensed, the sensuality of her, transporting me and her into plastic stone and back again to ungiving reality, subject and object made flesh and stone at once.

'Forgive me,' the man said, 'but have you been there?'

'There, where?' I asked, startled out of my reverie.

'Kejjuro?' He offered the word tentatively.

'Oh, Khajuraho, yes,' I replied, 'several times. My people come from a village close by.'

'Oh, really,' the woman exclaimed, her eyes lighting up. 'Perhaps you can tell us ... You see, my husband and I are thinking of going to India.'

'Yes, of course,' I interrupted, swept along by her reckless enthusiasm, 'with pleasure.'

'When, now?', she asked, eager as a child. 'In the café perhaps, over a cup of tea?'

'Really Suzanne,' the man chided her, 'the gentleman has probably not been through the exhibition yet.'

'No, no,' I protested, 'I have seen all I want to. Let's go. Incidentally, my name is Anand.'

'I am George, George Denning, and this is my wife, Suzanne.'

Over tea and cakes, we chatted about their impending trip to India. George, I gathered, was a playwright, though not a very successful one. Only one of his plays had ever been performed, and that by a student group. His wife, though, was a promising actress and had already played in the *Three Sisters* at the Royal Court. In which part I did not ask, but Masha, I thought, would have suited her well. She had the figure for it, and the rustle of autumn leaves in her voice, and large green eyes that threatened to drown you in pools of oblivion. I would not say she was beautiful, or attractive even, except for that quality of sensuality that hung about her like a perfume, not strong or heady but fugitive and enticing.

George was not bad-looking himself, tall and slim, with regular Anglo-Saxon features, but somewhat predatory. They were both good talkers and easy to be with — and, lost in talk of my country, I had lost all count of time, when something that George said suddenly reminded me that I was already half an hour late for my meeting with Nancy. I quickly took their telephone number (I didn't have one to give) and fled, promising to get in touch with them as soon as they returned from their Indian trip.

It was in the spring of 1969, almost a year after our first meeting, that I finally got round to ringing the Dennings. (My father had died in the meantime and I had had to return to India to settle some family matters.) George answered the phone but could not place me at first.

'Who? Anand? I am sorry but —'

'We met at the Indian exhibition ... Khajuraho?'

'Oh Anand, yes of course, Anand.' He had finally

located me and was trying to sound pleased and surprised. 'This is a pleasant surprise. Long time no see.'

I muttered something about having been away, but I don't think he was paying much attention to my explanation.

'Hey man,' he said, affecting a familiarity I would not have suspected of him, 'India was terrific. Why don't you come and see us? We are moving to a new flat in Hampstead. Will you give us a ring?'

'At the same number?' I inquired.

'Oh, no, I forgot. Why don't we ring you?'

I gave him my number (I had a telephone now).

I did not hear from them till the summer, and it was Sue who rang me then. She was sorry she couldn't get in touch earlier, she said, 'moving house and all that' – and, in any case, it was by accident that she had found my number on the telephone pad. George hadn't told her I had rung. Could I go to dinner with them, soon? There was so much she wanted to say, how much she and George owed me, that trip to India had made all the difference to George's writing. He was doing new things, getting atmosphere into his plays, and symbolism.

'You must talk to him about it,' she ended. 'I don't know what it's all about, but I figure in all of them.'

I demurred. George, it appeared, was on the way up and I doubted his wanting to discuss his plays with me. Khajuraho and India, perhaps, but that was in the past. Sue must have sensed my hesitation.

'You will come, won't you, next Thursday? And even if you don't want to talk to George – he is moody, you know what writers are like – I want to see you.'

And I knew she meant it, so I went.

But the dinner was a disaster, for me. There were too many people for one thing, and most of them writers and actors and artists, the up-and-coming variety, all of them bursting with enthusiasm and ideas and false bonhomie. I felt particularly vulnerable because every time George introduced me to someone, it was as 'the man who sent us to India', which made me feel like some sort of travel agent for avant-garde writers. Only Sue, amongst them all, treated me with genuine affection and friendship.

It was some six months before I saw George and Sue again, at the Hampstead Theatre Club where, attracted by 'rave reviews', I had gone to see George's first major play, *The Booth*. I was just leaving the theatre when a voice, all silk and paper, behind me said, 'Sneaking away, are you, after all this time?'

'Sue,' I turned around and spontaneously took her hands in mine as though we were long-lost friends: she commanded intimacy, and I had not got over her presence on the stage that evening.

'I was going to ring you, truly I was.'

'It doesn't matter,' she interrupted. 'You can make up for all that now. Come and have supper with us, at home, just us three. I am tired of all these parties, and you can tell us what you thought of the play.'

I did not want to discuss the play. There had been no play: just a telephone booth on a barren stage and three characters (Sue and two men) saying meaningless things to each other meaningfully, before they disappeared in turn into and out of the booth. What could I say about that? But I did not want to move out of Sue's orbit altogether, and so I fell in with her plans.

Their flat was a writer's flat, or what I imagined to be a writer's flat: a long rambling front room, with hanging carpets on the walls and lie-on cushions on the floor and folding divans, and arty-crafty things from India and, in the alcove on one wall, half in shadow, half in light, what looked like the embossed figures of the Khajuraho lovers. And from there you could see into the study, full of books and papers and magazines, with a curved table in a bay window, overlooking the green of the heath. There, at the table, it suddenly came to me irreverently, suspended between the green and the groin, was where the great man had written *The Booth*.

There was little of Sue in that flat, it was all George, except when Sue entered a room and filled it with her reluctant presence. Perhaps it was that that George fought against, surrounding himself with his things and stamping the place with his authority.

'Coffee?' Sue asked, clearing away the dishes, 'and brandy?'

'Yes, please,' I replied desperately. The moment had come when I was going to be asked about the play and I needed the brandy.

'So, what did you think of my play?' inquired George, offhandedly, as though to test my worth as a critic rather than his as a playwright.

'Well, George', I began haltingly, finishing my brandy and pouring myself another.

'Yes?'

'I liked it,' I lied. 'Yes, I liked it,' I repeated, hoping

that repetition would convey conviction.

'But why? What did it tell you?'

'Tell me?' I looked at Sue, sunk into a large cushion, for help. She smiled at me encouragingly. This was going to be worse than I thought. I had better make a clean breast of it. Of what? What had I done? I fortified myself with yet another brandy. But before I could say anything, George prodded me on towards his line of thinking.

'What about the atmosphere?' he asked helpfully.

'Atmosphere?' The brandy was going to my head and I was finding it difficult to follow him.

'Yes, the atmosphere of desolation, of a void, and people trying to reach out across it to each other.'

'Ah, yes. Yes, of course, there's that, there's certainly that.' It was easier to flow along with the tide.

'And the symbolism? Oh, come on, Anand, you of all people couldn't have failed to understand that.'

'Yes, the symbolism.' I remembered Sue had said something about it but, for the life of me, I could not recall what it was she had said.

'They are trying to reach out across this void, right?' George went on. I nodded earnestly. 'But they themselves are empty, as people, as individuals, they are de-void. See what I mean? De-void? And the only thing of significance is the phone booth. There at least there is life, communication, or at least the possibility, the hope of communication.'

'What about Sue?' I asked drunkenly.

'Suzanne? What has she got to do with it?'

I wagged my finger knowingly.

'What on earth are you on about?' George was angry. He had tried to explain his play, he said, for my sake, he said, because plays should never be explained; they were inexplicable, like life itself, and yet I had failed to grasp his meaning.

'Yes, Sue'. I pointedly refused to call her Suzanne, 'because without Sue there would be no play,' I went on brazenly. 'And no playwright.' I laughed uproariously, enjoying his dismay and my catharsis. 'And no visiting you and listening to your bullshit, either.' I laughed even louder and laughingly followed my laughter out of his house. And, as I left, I thought I saw a smile pucker Sue's lips.

'Come again,' she said, and then, in a whisper, 'and again.'

∝

I did not visit either of them after that. I saw them on TV, though, several times: Sue in his plays and he himself interviewed after every one of them. Gradually, it began to dawn on me that all George's plays revolved around that magic quality in Sue which exuded sex even as it withheld it, a nun-like sensuality that aroused eroticism only to assert its ascetic sublimation. It was a property that was uniquely Sue's, and George's genius was to make it into a theatrical property. And, however much that drained her of all her other talents and kept her own genius from flowering, she submitted herself, out of some incredible love that I could never understand, to every use of George's — and she knew it. I realize now that what I had said that night in drunken jest had carried more meaning than I had allowed it then.

George's plays were all the vogue for almost a decade. He was, said the critics, a philosopher-poet who brought to the theatre the emotional vacuity of our times and yet filled it with a sensuality that promised renewal. Then, suddenly, the plays ceased and George disappeared from view. When he re-emerged again a couple of years later with *The Cubicle* and *The Tree*, they turned out to be flops, and he himself sank without trace into that void he had so earnestly wanted to recapture. Sue was not in either of the plays; she had fallen out of the public eye altogether. George, I gathered, had left her at the height of his success and had married Fiona Garlick, the rich and fragrantly beautiful anti-porn campaigner.

I wondered what had happened to Sue. I had got her number from a mutual friend and had been meaning to ring her, but had kept putting it off with the idea of calling on her personally – when she appeared on TV again, in a third-rate play by an unknown writer, who had the merit, at least, of casting her in the more demanding role of a latter-day Hedda Gabler. She looked all haggard and worn, emptied, and did not carry conviction to the part.

As I went to visit her at her flat the following day, not even sure that she lived there any more, an old man in a shabby coat was coming out.

'Does Mrs Denning?' I began, 'Sue Denning, live –'

He shook his head and said in a broken voice. 'Dead, Sue is dead. The reviews killed her. She had nothing to give, they said.' He put his hand on my shoulder. 'The truth is, she had no one to give it to.'

Louise

He was looking forward to his visit. It was ten years to the day, almost, since he had first set eyes on her, April Fool's Day 1964 to be exact. She must have been in her forties even then, but strikingly attractive and immaculately groomed, and kept from time. Not even three husbands, and God knows how many lovers, had damped her fires: they remained bright and alight behind the large brown eyes, dammed up and waiting to be released again – though he did not know it then.

She had kindled him, so to speak, at a time when, consumed by a loveless marriage, he was all burnt out. She had roused him to her and to himself and, for a while, he felt he loved her.

And he probably had, so gentle she was and giving, a woman's woman, he had thought, unlike his wife who was all man and manager. She was interested, too, in the things he was interested in: music and reading and cricket. In fact, it was in the cricket section that he first came upon her as he was closing up the library for the night. Everybody else had gone.

'Sorry, we are closing,' he told her.

'Oh, are you?' She lifted her eyes from behind her half-moon glasses. 'I didn't realize it was so late. I don't suppose I could borrow this Wisden for a couple of days?'

'No, I am afraid not,' Kumar drawled out reluctantly. 'It's for reference only.'

'But it's not the current one,' she pointed out. 'There can't be a run on the market for an old...' She stopped on seeing his startled expression and laughed hilariously. 'I was only joking.'

Relieved, Kumar took the volume from her hand and examined it. 'You are quite right,' he said, with sudden authority. His boss had gone for the day and he was in charge. 'And it's Saturday. You can have it over the weekend. How's that?'

'That's lovely, thank you.'

He took the book to the counter and stamped it for her.

'Is this for your husband or your son?' he asked, finding no clue on the ticket which was in the name of L. C. Tate.

'It's for me,' she smiled. 'Why? Can't a woman be interested in cricket?'

'No, no, I am sorry, I didn't mean that. I meant ... why this particular volume?' Kumar ended weakly.

'Because I want to read about the great Ranji. My father knew him, you know, in India, and saw him play —'

'Did he?' Kumar leapt in. 'So did my father, when he was a boy. Ah, Ranjitsinhji.' He shook his head from side to side, 'Yes, he was the greatest. Such fluency, such timing, it was like a morning raga, my father used to say, the improvisation, the timing...' He handed the book over to her. 'Good-night, Mrs Tate. It was nice talking to you.'

'Call me Louise. And you are?'

'Kumar.'

'Well, Kumar, we should continue our chat some-time. Perhaps you'll come and take tea with me. Next Saturday?'

'I would love to. Thanks.' He pointed to the address on the ticket. 'Here?'

'Yes, that's my address. My husband is away at week-ends, playing in some cricket match or other.'

That had been the first of many Saturday teas. Louise was a great talker, and Kumar had an hour or two to spare before he went home to his wife's regimen. Besides, 'taking tea' was exactly what it was, as elabo-rate and elegant and English an affair as Kumar had come to expect from all that he had read in the novels of Jane Austen and Henry James.

Louise herself was a tall, slim, elegant woman, with a figure and looks that made no concession to age ex-cept for the silvering hair gathered in a bun on the nape of her neck.

The drawing-room in which they took tea was large and comfortable. It had a music console in one corner and, at the opposite end, a baby grand, on which was as-sembled an array of framed photographs, which Kumar later came to discover were those of her husbands and children and grandchildren. Louise herself did not play the piano (her daughters had) but she listened avidly to the Third Programme and often had a record on her player when Kumar went to visit her, usually a piece of religious music that they had together discovered on one of their regular visits to the music library. It was there, one day, in the middle of the Benedictus from Haydn's Little Organ Mass, that Kumar had ventured to plant a kiss on the back of her ear.

'No don't,' she had reacted. 'Please. Not you.'

But, when he went to visit her the following Saturday, with a bunch of roses by way of apology, she embraced him warmly and, taking the flowers from his hand, kissed him full on the mouth. Kumar was startled, but she only laughed at his discomfiture and led him into the drawing-room. The curtains were already drawn, although it was only six o'clock of a late summer evening, and a soft fire danced in the fireplace. A rhumba beat out its seductive rhythm on the record-player.

Louise put the flowers in a vase and took it over to the mantelpiece and, as she stood there, silhouetted against the flickering flames of the fire, in a diaphanous dress with nothing beneath, she looked to Kumar like something out of Botticelli, fresh and young as spring. He flushed and looked away, and looked back again, unable to take his eyes off her.

Louise finished arranging the flowers and, shaking her hair loose to fall straight and silvery-bright below her shoulders, she came and sat beside Kumar on the sofa. He pulled her to him and kissed her. She drew back and, then, suddenly threw herself on him, covering his face with kisses, taking his mouth into hers, and tugging feverishly at his trousers. And, as Kumar struggled for breath, she took her mouth below and was about to take him in when he broke loose and fled, his trousers clutched in his hand.

He had not seen her since then, but he could still recall the storm of emotions that had racked him on his way home that day. He felt hurt, disappointed, sullied ... How could she ... theirs was not that kind of love ... he had not slept with anyone but his wife and that had been arranged ... the marriage, anyway ... by his parents ... in a hurry to break him of his love for a Muslim girl ... and pack him off to England to do a course in accountancy ... all that was in the dowry ... and he had given up his love reluctantly ... to see the mother country ... the country of Jane Austen, Virginia Woolf, Anthony Trollope, go to plays and concerts, see the Houses of Parliament, Hyde Park, Leicester Square.

But, taken up with finding England, he had failed his exams, and his wife, cheated of her dowry rights, had turned even more ungiving and bitter. And then Louise ... Louise ... his first love come alive again ... his first unspeakable, unreachable love ... reborn, here, in the country of his mind. He was in love with her and England.

It was not like her, not the Louise he knew ... his Louise ... what on earth was she thinking of ... perhaps he had provoked her ... on the contrary ... and in that dress ... and the way she had gone for him. God, what an escape, she would have swallowed him up, eaten him, she probably ate all her men. A man-eater, that's what she really was, a man-eater. To be castrated by his wife or be devoured by Louise, what a choice! All those husbands of hers, she must have swallowed them all up and her lovers, they were not around any more, John, Bill, Mike, Sam, where were they – only their photographs remained.

There was still Pat, though. He was still around. Pat Tate, the third (or fourth?) husband. Kumar had met him just that once when rain had washed out play. Patrick was home that Saturday, practising his cover drive in the drawing-room when Kumar arrived.

'Ha, ha, the man himself,' he greeted Kumar. 'Louise's pet librarian.' He shook Kumar's hands warmly. 'No offence, old boy. Just my little joke, you know. Sit down, sit down, Louise will be down soon.'

'No cricket, then?' Kumar asked weakly. Louise had not warned him that her husband would be home that day or that he looked nothing like his photograph, which was that of a slim, young lieutenant. This man was large and florid and dressed in cricketing flannels and a sweater with the MCC crest on it.

'What, in this rain?' he guffawed. 'Not likely, old boy, not likely. I have been on at the blokes at the Club to get an indoor what-you-may-call-it, but no spondulicks.' He picked up his bat from the piano. 'I was just practising my cover drive when you came.' He positioned himself in front of an imaginary wicket. 'You don't mind, do you?'

'No, not at all, not at all.'

Patrick rehearsed the stroke a few times, with Kumar looking interestedly on.

'How on earth does he do it? It's my follow-through, you know. Sobers I mean. Do you play?'

'Not now. I played for my College XI back home.'

'Where's that? Bombay?' Kumar nodded. 'I was there during the war, defending the Raj and all that. Do you ... ah, here you are dear.' He broke off as Louise came in. 'I was just telling —'

'So you two have finally met,' Louise observed flatly.

'Oh, yes, we had a capital chat, what?' Patrick placed his bat behind the door and looked at his watch. 'I'm sorry, dear, but I've got to tootle along to the Club. I told the boys —'

'Yes, yes, go.'

'Cheerio, old boy.' He shrugged himself into a blazer and held out his hand to Kumar. 'I am sorry I didn't offer you a drink, but my wife will look after you, I am sure.' And he grinned as he left.

Kumar had not set much store by his remark at the time. But knowing what he knew now, he was certain that there had been a wink and a nod behind that grin. The man did not care about his wife at all, only his cricket. No wonder Louise had not been able to gobble him up. He was an Englishman after all, out of Harrow and Cambridge and the British Empire, unswallowable. Even so, she would have devoured him at the last, except that his only passion was cricket. He probably went to bed in his pads and his cricket cap and, presumably, in his codpiece too. It was that, perhaps, that kept him from being devoured — nibbled at, maybe, but undevoured.

He should be more like Patrick, thought Kumar, aloof, indifferent, a man of the world. That way he wouldn't get hurt, that way he might even learn to live with his wife. What he could not do was to go on being everybody's door-mat. All his life he had been acted upon. No more. Everyone took advantage of him – his parents, his wife, his boss, Louise. He had been a dutiful son, a faithful husband, a loyal worker, a chaste lover. But no more, he swore, no more. From now on, he was going to live it up.

And he had, but only after his wife, unable to make a success of him, had taken what was left of her dowry and gone back home. He had gone into the import-export business after that, with his cousin, and become rich and fat and promiscuous.

Louise had started it all, and here she was again, after all these years, asking to see him, just once more, for old time's sake. Patrick had taken everything she had, she wrote, and thrown her out of the house. She was alone and bereft of everyone, incarcerated in a guest-house with the old and the decrepit. He must come to her, he was her only friend.

He could not refuse her. She had never asked anything of him before, and he was in a position to repay some of her past kindnesses. In fact, he was pleased she had asked him and not all those other men or her countless children, scattered all over the globe. They must have all left her, taken what she had to give and left her. She had been treated ill by the world, she needed succour, and who but him ... and especially now when she was grown old and poor and lonely.

Her voice on the phone that night, when he had rung to say that he was coming to see her the following day, was as vibrant and pulsating as ever he had known it to be. Only now, it excited him sexually. He had always wondered what it would have been like with her if he had not fled that day.

'You sound as young as ever,' he had teased her, and she had rejoined that she might be down but not out and, rising to his appreciation, had promised to teach him a thing or two. To which he had replied that they would see, tomorrow, who taught whom.

But, as she stood before him on the station platform, reeking of expensive perfume, her grey hair lacquered down and electric with excitement − her hair, she had once declared, was her most erogenous zone − her once tall figure wrinkled smaller, he felt cheated again. And he thought to go, give her some money and go.

'No, don't,' she said, sensing his disappointment. 'I didn't want you for that. I never did. But I never got a chance to tell you. That's why I wanted to see you.' She led him to a bench and sat him down beside her. 'You see, my dear, nobody ever loved me the way you did. All they ever wanted was sex. I always seemed to get them that way, I don't know why, and so I played up to them. That way, at least, I could have the rest of me to myself. No, let me go on. So when you kissed me tenderly that day in the music library ... You see, I thought you were different, you loved me, for myself, but the next time you kissed me, that last day, I thought you were after the same thing − and, like a habit, I gave in. That was what I had always been used to, with all those others, that was what was expected of me. It was only when you had gone −'

He took her hands in his and kissed them.

'I am here now,' he said.

The Dream Train

I knew, as though in a dream, that there was a college somewhere, and I had taught there, been happy there, and loved the people who taught with me. But I didn't know where.

There was a train I had to take. There was only one train in the town. I took it, not knowing in which direction I should go.

There was a man and a child on the train. He was teaching her sums. I didn't know where to get off. I got off when they did.

They sat on a bank by the railway line, teaching and learning, loath to let go of each other's task and the sunlight.

Was there a school somewhere here? I asked him. On a hill, perhaps, sort of square — my memory was coming back — or maybe rectangular, stretched across.

Yes, he said, there it is.

And there it was, on the other side of the bank we sat on, way above in the hills. I could see it clearly now and I remembered the green slope up which I had walked so many times.

The building was dilapidated, the room deserted. I climbed the stairs to where I thought I had my class. I heard the voices of children, but I could not see them.

I looked out of the window. Yes, that was the hill I climbed every morning to the school.

I heard voices and I turned round to see two women talking.

I used to teach here, I said by way of explanation, wasn't this a school ... Yes, they said, but it's moved down there into the town below.

I turned to go and saw a man with a sheaf of papers in his hand. I remembered him. David.

Hello, Vikram, he said, matter-of-factly, clasping my hand in a grip I knew so well.

You remember me then?

Of course. She's down there in the school.

I walked down the street and, as I passed the shoe-shop, someone called to me.

Hey, Vikram.

I went in. It was Sam. He was not drunk. He was not unkempt. He was neatly dressed in spotless white trousers and shirt, hair neatly combed back. He did not look like someone who was going to touch me for money, tell me dirty stories in exchange.

I left my wife, he said. I nodded.

I am looking for –

Yes, over there, behind the market.

I hesitated.

She's there, I saw her. This morning.

I hurried across the square and entered the school. But there was no receptionist, no office, no one, no place I could ask. I must have come in through the wrong door.

I drifted past the empty classrooms and out into

the quadrangle. Someone was hurrying past — the same, slim, hurrying figure, straight now as ever, her crow-black hair turned early grey.

I ran after her, caught up and turned her around.

Still in a hurry, I said.

Vikram, you have come.

Sisters

Miriam was glad they were coming to stay with her. Even at such short notice. Eileen who was going to put them up had cried off at the last moment; she had to put up her sister instead, she said. But Miriam was not put out. All she had to do was to borrow an extra bed from her sister-in-law and put it in the spare room. Karen and Flora would be no trouble. They were probably used to roughing it anyway, having spent all that time in Pakistan. Karen had been there five years earlier with her husband, Ibrahim, and had got used to the simple life, but it could not have made much difference to their daughter, Flora, who could not have been more than eight or nine at the time. Ibrahim himself was a simple, plain-living man, as befitted a scholar and an activist, he would say, and their flat in New York was by no means luxurious.

No, they should be no trouble, Miriam reassured herself, rummaging in her bag for her ticket as the train drew up at Warren Street station. In fact, she was looking forward to comparing notes with Karen. Miriam's husband, Mohan, was from Sri Lanka and Miriam herself had been to the island a number of times and become partial to its way of life. A place, for her, was its people – and the people there, though mostly poor and often temperamental, were not grasping or mean or inhospitable. They gave of what little they had, freely, without counting the cost. Maybe it was a quality that came of living in extended families. And, untidy and messy though this sometimes seemed to her, there was more perhaps to be said for it than for nuclear families doing their nuclear things in their nuclear homes, sanitized from the rub of life.

Karen had probably experienced the same sort of thing, thought Miriam, as she hurried along to work. Karen, of course, could go and live in Pakistan if and when Ibrahim chose to do so, whereas Miriam's hopes of ever settling down in Sri Lanka had vanished when civil war had broken out there and her husband had become a political exile. But the legacy of the people she had known remained with her still, in her work at the community centre and the open house she kept. She was not the type of person who was given to nostalgia and she was glad for Karen that her husband could go back to Pakistan. Ibrahim's political activities were still too scholastic to invoke the wrath of Zia's military government.

Two days before Karen was due to arrive, Mohan slipped a disc. It was a recurring complaint of his, and one he was beginning to cope with, but this time it took him bad. His back seized up completely on the second day and he became bed-ridden.

Miriam was not unduly concerned, though. Mohan could now be persuaded to take up his writing again: the events in Sri Lanka had claimed all his attention and his work on behalf of the refugees had claimed all his time. Even the articles he had been commissioned to write had withered on the vine.

Besides, she too needed a holiday from work. She could look after Mohan and have more time for Karen at the same time: they were here only for a week, after all, and part of that time Karen wanted to spend in 'Hardy country'. Miriam's only regret was that she could not go to the coach terminus to fetch them.

It was a long July evening, the sun had broken out at last after unending days of cold and rain, and Miriam had hurried through her chores to be ready to receive her visitors. Mohan's muscles had been in spasm throughout the day and the doctor had recommended hot and cold compresses every four hours. Miriam had just finished 'doing him' for the evening when Karen phoned from the airport. The plane had been delayed in Karachi for over two hours, and they had only just arrived. She had tried Miriam's office but there was no reply; she was glad she had caught Miriam at home.

'I am sorry, Karen,' Miriam replied, 'but you'll have to take a taxi all the way here. Or come by coach and tube if you haven't much luggage. Mohan's in bed with a bad back.'

'Oh dear, that's terrible. No, no, don't worry about us. We'll find our way. But are you sure you can manage? We don't want to give you more trouble.'

'Don't be silly,' Miriam reassured her. 'It's only for a few days, and Mohan won't have it otherwise, for Ibrahim's sake, if not yours.'

'OK then, but only if you are sure ... and in any case we'll be out most of the time. Flora has some friends from New York she's dying to see and I want to go to the Yorkshire moors.'

'I thought it was Hardy —'

'Yes, but Flora . . . I'll tell you when I see you.'

Miriam put the phone down and went upstairs to Mohan.

'That was Karen. She was ever so sorry about your back, thought she was imposing on us. You see, you were wrong to worry. I think she is very considerate like that.'

'Yes, you are right,' replied Mohan. 'It was she who sent me that Canadian lumber-jacket through Ibrahim; he had forgotten that I had looked for one all over New York.'

A few minutes later, the phone rang again. It was Karen. She was not sure what she should do. It would cost her the earth to leave all her bags at the airport for a week. Would a taxi to Kingsbury be cheaper?

'Quite a bit,' Miriam replied. 'Take a taxi then, it will be quicker anyway, and you must be tired.'

Miriam went up to the bedroom to report to Mohan, who felt cruelly cut off from the world and its events every time he took to bed.

'She is not a spend-thrift, is she?' Mohan asked and added laughingly, 'like you.'

Miriam hit him playfully and he tried to reach out for her, but the pain held him back.

'At least they'll be here before the dinner gets cold,' replied Miriam and went off to make it.

✌

'Haa-ie,' Mohan heard Karen call out enthusiastically

as Miriam opened the door to her. 'How *are* you?' The emphasis was unmistakable. 'Is Mohan all right?' The concern rang true.

'No, not really. Gosh, how Flo has grown,' Miriam remarked.

'Yes, hasn't she?' Karen looked proudly at her daughter and then, sidling up to Miriam, 'She likes to be called by her full name,' she said in a stage whisper. 'Florah, with an h at the end, mind,' and she laughed playfully.

Her face was not right any more for that sort of humour, Miriam could not help thinking: it had grown gaunt and white and anxious, and her hair was grey beyond her years. Perhaps the humour had remained, if humour it was, when everything else had left her.

'Where is he?' she asked.

Miriam pointed upwards and conducted Karen to Mohan's bedroom.

'Haiee,' she greeted him, 'how *are* you? Bad huh?'

'Hello, Karen. I'm OK, but you must be tired and hungry. Why don't you ... Hello Flo,' he broke off as the daughter came into the room. 'Flo-rah,' whispered Miriam in his ear. 'OK, Florah then, but you still have that smile. Sit down, sit down.' He remembered her for the open smile and the side-long glance with which she used to disarm him as a child. Her father on his visits to London had kept Mohan posted on Florah's academic brilliance and her particular sharpness of mind.

'You must tell me how you liked Pakistan,' he said. Florah nodded sagely and smiled innocently. 'Tomorrow, then. You'll want to eat and go to bed now.'

Karen, who had left the room as Mohan was talking to Florah, now came back with a sarong.

'Ibrahim sent you this,' she said, and went on before Mohan could say anything, 'Isn't it gorgeous?'

Mohan didn't think so but raised himself up to look at the heavy, gaudy bit of cloth, more like a bedspread than a sarong, a little closer. He was sure Karen had chosen it. Ibrahim and he never gave each other presents.

'Be careful,' warned Miriam.

'No, no, you are not to move,' admonished Karen.

'You see what I mean, Karen,' Miriam turned to her friend. 'He won't be still.'

'Is there anything I can do?'

'We can keep him tied down,' she replied and then turning to her husband, 'there are two of us now, Mohan, sisterhood is powerful.'

'Three,' corrected Karen.

It was two days before Mohan began to twig that something had gone wrong with sisterhood. Strain his ears as he would, he could not catch what was going on in the rest of the house, small though it was. Karen dropped in on him only for a minute or two in the mornings when Miriam was out, and Florah would waft in when she found that she had misplaced her mother. Or that was how she came across to Mohan, for all the interest she showed in him or in the conversations he tried to strike up with her. Perhaps she was shy and reserved, though he couldn't help hearing her chattering away with her mother in the next room or, more often, to her friends on the telephone. They seemed always to be making appointments to see people, but never went anywhere.

The strain was beginning to show on Miriam. Mohan felt bad that she should have to look to all his needs – fetching his bedpan, feeding him, clearing the mess – while not getting in the way of Karen's and Florah's ablutions (there was only one toilet and bathroom) without having to see they were looked after too.

'Why don't they go out?' Mohan asked her.

'Oh, it's not their fault. Eileen keeps postponing their visit to her, she has a baby now, and that other woman in Tunbridge Wells is out hay-making or something whenever Karen rings.'

'But you can't be cooking for them all the time, and you seem to be going to the shops every day.'

'No, it's only the evening meal. And I cook for us anyway.'

'Why can't she –'

'Well she keeps offering...' Miriam could not hide the look of disappointment on her face. 'And, yes, I must tell them about the shopping. They have finished everything in the larder. I don't mind their taking the stuff if they tell me. That's why I didn't give you corn-flakes today. The milk is all gone. I asked Karen to tell me in time to order more milk. And the eggs ... I got an extra pint today,' Miriam was close to tears, 'and when I went down, it was finished. Karen says Florah had not seen cow's milk in Pakistan, only goat's, and she is making up for it now. So how can I say anything?'

'I'll speak to Karen,' Mohan promised her. 'Perhaps she doesn't understand our problems. It's a good thing you don't have to go to work as well,' he muttered to himself.

But try as he might, Mohan could not get through to Karen, perhaps because what he wanted to stress was not the demands that all of them were making on Miriam, but Miriam's inability to say no to them.

'She has to look after everybody,' Mohan explained laughingly, 'do everything herself. And you have seen what it is like: my sister-in-law and her plumbing, that woman over the road and her marital problems, all that trouble in the office (they can't make a bloody decision without her) — and me in bed, useless to help.'

Karen nodded vehemently. 'Yes, we came at a bad time, and one week is too much.' She paused. 'Do you want us to move out?'

'That's not what I am saying at all,' replied Mohan hotly. 'That's a typical American answer.' Karen looked alarmed.

'European, then, western. Oh, I don't know. The point is not to reduce our relationships to a manageable size but to increase ourselves to accommodate a hundred relationships — be considerate, sensitive, thoughtful, that sort of thing...' He trailed off as Karen began nodding at his every word.

'Yes, you are right. I am going to Wales at the weekend for a couple of days and Florah is going to a friend. So...' She broke off as Miriam came in and, turning to her, said, 'Can I go to the store for you for anything?'

'The shops are closed,' Miriam remarked indifferently. She obviously did not connect Karen's intentions with her words.

'Oh well then, I'll make something for dinner.' Karen stood up from the bed. 'Spaghetti?'

'Mohan can't eat it, remember I told you — his stomach...' Miriam was clearly tiring of the conversation. 'I'm making kedgeree, anyway, and it's no trouble making it for two more. Your nephew isn't taking you out, I suppose?'

'No, something seems to have come up,' Karen replied and, hearing Florah call for her, left the room.

'Sorry, love, I just couldn't get through,' apologized Mohan despondently.

Miriam sat down beside him and took his hand. 'Never mind, we'll have some peace at the weekend.'

'There's not much sisterhood there, you know,' Mohan remarked, 'I don't think Pakistan taught her much.'

Miriam nodded. She looked sad and far away.

'How could it?' Mohan went on, 'They lived in Rafique's house with his three wives and umpteen servants. You know, that immensely rich guy, barrister or something, who dabbles in national politics. Ibrahim's friend. How could —'

'Oh, for God's sake, stop getting worked up about them,' Miriam shouted at him quietly. 'They are not a bother, you are. What's that?' she broke off, as a smell of cooking wafted up the stairs, 'something's burning' and she rushed down to the kitchen.

She was up again a few minutes later.

'You won't believe this,' she said, 'They are cooking spaghetti, for themselves.'

'But you said —'

'Yes, but Florah probably wanted spaghetti. And they have ruined my new breadboard, cut onions on it. The chopping board was there right in front of them. They don't even ask.'

She made a face and Mohan tweaked her nose, and suddenly she brightened up.

'The funny thing was that I was surprised to see the spaghetti and thought Karen had gone to the shops yesterday and I felt terrible I'd wronged her, but of course she had dug it out from the larder somewhere.'

'Please, no grumbles about food.'

'No, of course not. It's only for two more days. Tomorrow and the day after, they are in Wales.'

Later that evening, Karen developed a headache and a temperature. It looked as though the trip was off. Florah hadn't wanted to go anyway, and Karen was doubtful that she herself would be well enough to make the coach journey the following day. She kept taking her temperature every half hour — in her anxiety, Miriam thought, to make the trip. But when she was still taking her temperature throughout the following day and kept to her bed, except at meal times, Miriam decided that she was just a hypochondriac.

Mohan was not convinced. 'Maybe that too, but it's also Florah. When she didn't want to go —'

'Yes, I think you are right.' Miriam interrupted, 'Everything's for Florah. Where are all the friends Karen was going to see? Why didn't Eileen put them up? All that stuff about Eileen's sister coming, I now understand, was not correct: she had come and gone. Actually, I think Karen broke journey here so that Florah could see her friends from New York. She keeps saying how Florah missed them when she was in Pakistan.'

'I'll have another go at her,' Mohan promised. 'At least get her to go out somewhere, get out from under our feet.'

'I suggested they go to Kenwood House, maybe take in the Sunday concert in the open air, it's such fine weather, if she is better, that is.'

'She will be, if Florah has nothing else to do. You said her friend had gone out of London.'

After dinner that night, Mohan invited Karen into his room for a chat.

He sat her beside him on his bed and began warmly.

'Karen, if we are friends — at least we owe that much to Ibrahim — we must be able to talk frankly. Yes?'

Karen nodded vehemently, as was her way, with short, sharp, staccato nods.

'How are you feeling, anyway?' inquired Mohan, belatedly.

'My temperature is down from 99.5 to close to normal, but I've still got a headache.'

Mohan laughed at the accuracy of the statistics. 'You are a bit of a hypochondriac, aren't you, Karen?' he teased her. 'Incidentally there was nothing wrong with Florah, was there?'

'No, no, the doctor said it was just a swollen gland, from the mosquito bites.'

'I told you so, didn't I?'

'Yes, but it's always good to check these things, especially when you come from places like Pakistan.'

Mohan tried another tack.

'I am glad you showed us your review article,' he said, picking it up and the book of photographs from his bedside table. 'It is very insightful, the way you see pictures, I mean. You must get it published.'

'It's worth publishing, you think?'

'It certainly is. It shows great sensitivity and understanding of the native Americans, like that piece you did for the *Voice* on America in Vietnam.'

Karen was pleased. Mohan was a good critic and an honest one. Ibrahim trusted his judgement too.

'But how is it,' Mohan went on boldly, 'that that sensibility does not come into your everyday life?'

He saw that he had shocked Karen, upset her even, and quickly moved his argument to another level.

'Perhaps it's a western thing again, this business of keeping your emotions, your sensibilities, for art, literature, that sort of thing?'

Karen seemed a bit more comfortable now that the discussion was not pointed at her.

'No, I don't think so. It's just that we don't show it.'

Mohan had the feeling that, however sharp he was, he was not going to get his teeth into Karen. It was not that she was evasive so much as uninterested, uncritical of herself, self-centred. No, that was not right: she was centred on Florah, and everybody else came after.

'Perhaps I put it badly,' suggested Mohan. 'What I was getting at was not the style of relating to people but that ... I don't know how to put it. Surely, it is only by relating to people openly, unselfishly, that our sensibilities are sharpened and that in turn opens us out to people. No?'

Karen looked blank, and Mohan decided to jump in with both feet.

'Look, all I am saying is that my love for my child should open me out to all the children in the world, my love for my wife should open me out to all the women. I don't mean ... well, you know what I mean.'

Karen nodded, slowly this time, and Mohan was encouraged to go on.

'But love is also about justice: what is owed to my child, my woman, and what is owed to me. To love someone beyond their due is to be unjust to oneself and therefore not only to others but to the person you love.'

Karen had stopped nodding.

'You can't go on loving Florah at your expense,' Mohan finally blurted out. 'You are too protective of her, you give into her every whim and fancy. There's nothing of yourself that you keep for yourself, least of all for other people. Isn't that true?'

'You don't understand,' Karen protested. 'Florah had a very bad time in Pakistan. She felt wrenched – from New York, from her friends. Six weeks is a long time.'

'Oh?'

'For a young girl, I mean. She is not sure how they'll see her now. She is anxious. She is in pain.'

'But pain is a good thing,' Mohan said gently. 'I don't mean we've got to go and seek it ... but surely it is through pain that we grow. And in any case, you can't protect her from –'

'Yes, I know that, but it's not easy for her. It's like the time I went back to the States after working for the peace corps in Africa. I had nothing in common with my friends any more.'

'That's good, that's tremendous. Why shouldn't we outgrow people? If Pakistan meant anything, Florah will certainly have outgrown her friends; or, at least, she'll challenge them to keep up with her. You must give her air.' Mohan went on, emboldened by his self-appointed mission. 'Let her breathe. Let her make her own mistakes, and if you really love her you'll go through them yourself, don't suffocate her and yourself. Everything does not have to begin and end with Florah.'

Karen seemed to go along with the general tenor of Mohan's talk but felt it did not apply to Florah. It was her own fault, anyway ...

'I am not talking about you and Florah really,' interrupted Mohan, 'I didn't mean to. How can I? I don't know you that well and I don't know your relationship with your daughter. I wouldn't dare. I was talking generally, philosophically, if you like, and it is up to you to measure it against the touchstone of your own life and reject whatever doesn't ring true.'

Karen seemed able to accept that much and, on the

strength of it, Mohan managed to persuade her that both he and Miriam (whose relationship had been wearing thin these last few days) would like a little time to themselves. Perhaps Karen and Florah could go out for the day.

'Oh yes, we intend to,' Karen replied, 'now that I am better.' She wanted Mohan to know that it was her temperature that had kept her from venturing out. 'Florah and I are going to Eileen's for dinner,' she added, for good measure.

'You are finally going to see her, are you?'

'Yes. I know. She's like that. A bit iffy.'

'A bit what?'

'Iffy. You know, iffy.'

But at noon the next day, Karen and Florah were still pottering around the house.

'What's going on?' enquired Mohan of Miriam. 'I refuse to be marooned in this bed any longer,' he cried out in frustration.

'Florah gets up late, and then takes three hours to get ready, that's what's going on. And if you get out of that bed, I'm leaving the house, I mean it, I have had enough, between you and them and keeping you from them. I can't any more.' Miriam stormed out of the room.

She came up again a quarter of an hour later, calmer, and tried to pacify Mohan.

'They'll be going out soon. Karen asked me about pub lunches and things. Just imagine, peace for a whole day.'

'Whole day? Half the day is gone. They take the

sun so cavalierly. OK, OK,' Mohan added, 'I'll calm down. But seriously, now that I can get to the lavatory, can't I come down to watch Wimbledon? I want to see the McEnroe match. I can lie on the sofa.'

Miriam was about to be persuaded when the phone rang and she left the room.

'Who was that?' Mohan asked her when she returned a few minutes later.

'It was for them, it always is, but they never answer the phone. That's being polite, I suppose.' Miriam was unusually petty.

'What's the matter now?' Mohan pressed her to find the real cause of her anger.

'She's making sandwiches, tuna sandwiches to take for their lunch, cheaper than eating out I expect. I was saving it for your dinner, but you can have the kedgeree left over from last night.'

'What?' Mohan yelled, trying to get out of bed. 'Is there no limit to their inconsideration? I am going to ... there's a limit —' he spluttered.

'Stop it,' Miriam shouted back, 'stop it, and get back into bed. It is you who keep saying she is Ibrahim's wife and you owe it to Ibrahim.'

Mohan subsided, defeated, helpless. 'Yes, you are right. I can't fall out with him, I can't hurt him. He has done so much for us. And he's so thoughtful and generous. How does he ... Oh, I suppose husbands are blind,' he ended lamely.

'And fathers?' prompted Miriam.

After Karen and Florah had finally gone, Mohan inched his way down the stairs to watch the tennis on the box. But the day was so fine that he preferred to spend it lying on the sun-bed in the garden.

'It's nice to know I can walk again,' he said ruefully to Miriam, 'and look at this sun, after all these weeks of rain.'

'Yes, peaceful. Isn't my garden nice? I haven't had time —'

'Forget them. Enjoy your peace while you can.'

The peace did not last very long, for by six o'clock mother and daughter returned.

'Haiee,' said Karen and, seeing that Mohan was downstairs too, watching television, 'Wow,' she exclaimed.

Mohan and Miriam were too surprised to say anything, and mother and daughter passed them by without another word to the kitchen and the fridge.

Mohan turned to Miriam and asked to be helped upstairs. 'They get under my feet,' he explained. 'I am happier locked up in my room. It's only two more days.'

'Two and a half,' Miriam corrected, and they both burst out laughing. 'Have we really come to this?' she asked.

On their way through the kitchen, Mohan saw Karen chopping up some courgettes and could not help blurting out, 'I thought you were going out to dinner?'

Karen was taken aback. 'To Eileen's you mean? She put it off for tomorrow. We still might go out to a restaurant though.' She seemed genuinely caught in two minds and Mohan felt he could be blunt with her.

'Karen, Miriam has to go to work tomorrow. I can move about now and don't need her, and besides I want some peace. I expect you'll be out tomorrow?'

Karen could not mistake the drift of Mohan's talk.

'Oh, yes, Florah is going to Cambridge to see another friend who has just come from New York, and I'll go to see Eileen.'

A couple of hours later, Mohan looked out of his bedroom window to see Karen and Florah actually go out.

'Miriam,' he called out, 'they are not going for dinner, are they?'

'Yes they are,' replied Miriam rushing up the stairs. 'I think you got through to Karen at last, or perhaps she knows there's nothing in the house to eat, except her left-over spaghetti and the soup.'

But half an hour later they were back. Karen had not been able to find an Indian restaurant and none of the half dozen others − Greek, Italian, Chinese, Pizza, Kentucky Chicken, hamburger, fish and chips − would do.

'It would be quite funny,' Miriam came up to report, 'except that they are laying into the kedgeree I kept for your dinner.'

'Not food again, please, Miriam. You didn't say anything to them, did you?'

'Yes, of course I did. She asked me whether I minded and I said no, it's all right, Mohan can eat bread.'

'I am not hungry.'

'. . . and he's not hungry.' Miriam ended.

Mohan smiled and shrugged his shoulders.

'Can I have some bread then and some instant soup, not her rubbish?'

'Yes, when they have finished.'

When Miriam was leaving for work the following

morning, Karen was preparing to go to the shops. Florah had already gone to Cambridge.

'I am going to the stores,' announced Karen, 'to get some of the things you seem to have run out of. Is there anything else you want?'

'No, just get the things you need. I won't be going to the shops again till Wednesday. Ah yes, just a packet of bran cakes, for Mohan. We have run out.'

'I am sorry. Florah took a great liking to them She ate the last one.'

When Miriam returned home that evening, she found Karen in bed.

'What happened?' she asked Mohan. 'Didn't she —'

'She went to the shops, came back, ate something and took to bed. Says she's got a headache.'

'What about dinner at Eileen's?'

'She had to cancel it, Florah wasn't going anyway, it looks. Leave it,' he added, 'I have come to terms with it now.'

'I'll go and see how she is,' said Miriam, leaving the room. She came back a few minutes later.

'She does have a slight temperature,' she told Mohan. 'I said I'll cook something for all of us. What's to be done, she's such a hypochondriac and I feel sorry for her, like she was an elder sister.'

A couple of hours later all her goodwill had gone. Karen and Florah had finished their dinner, and Miriam had gone downstairs to fetch Mohan's and hers, only to come rushing up again, her face contorted in anger.

'They have pitched into Sasha's chocolates. It's almost all gone.'

'What?' Mohan went mad. 'That poor child.' Sasha, his grand-daughter, was half-blind and half-crippled, and she loved the chocolates a friend had brought back from Belgium, and he eked them out to her to eke out her love. 'That's it,' he yelled, hopping around the room in helpless anger. 'How can she be so bloody inconsiderate?'

'It was Florah,' Miriam explained, 'and she stopped when I told her about Sasha.'

Mohan quietened down finally. 'It's OK,' he said. 'I'm fine. I have paid Ibrahim back in full. If his wife and daughter don't care about him, why should I? That's it, no more.'

On the following day, Karen decided that she would stay in bed so that she'd be well enough to travel the day after. Miriam and Mohan hastened to agree. But when Miriam had gone to work, Karen went down to the phone and summoned Eileen and Ibrahim's nephew to her bedside.

Eileen finally turned up with husband and child for five minutes: the baby should not catch Karen's 'virus'. And the nephew turned up at eleven that night when everyone was in bed.

Mohan was just falling asleep when he was woken by the ring on the bell, and, opening his bedroom window, called out angrily into the night, 'Who's there?'

'It is me, Firoz,' replied a voice, 'come to see Karen and Florah.'

'What time do you think this is?' Mohan expostulated. 'They have gone to bed.'

'Leave it then,' said the man indifferently.

'Nope. Now that you have disturbed me, you can jolly well disturb them too. I'll go and wake them.'

Karen was surprised. She had told Mohan that it was unnecessary to open the door if Firoz came after they had all gone to bed. It was a decision that she had apparently taken against her daughter's wishes – as was now confirmed by Florah's triumphant leap down the stairs to welcome her cousin.

The next morning Miriam remarked to Karen, with a warmth reserved for tiresome guests who were about to depart, that Firoz should not have woken her up, she needed all the sleep she could get before a long journey, and she having been so ill. (And Miriam was not being sarcastic.)

Karen might have agreed with her but Florah broke in with 'it wasn't that late' (continuing her conversation with her mother it seemed) and her mother agreed with alacrity and was relieved when there was a ring on the door.

'That will be the taxi now,' she said, 'We'll go and say goodbye to Mohan.'

Mohan winced as Karen came up and thanked him, apologizing for any trouble they might have caused, and froze into rigor mortis as Florah tried to kiss him goodbye. The girl had had no relationship with him at all, though he had tried. She had not even bothered to be friendly to his little nieces who had visited him almost daily. She had, for a whole week, brought Mohan and Miriam to their knees, imprisoned them in their own home while exiling them from their domicile, and not even directly but through her mother, and she through a surrogate Ibrahim, and here she was trying to wipe the slate clean with a kiss, while her mother looked on approvingly.

Miriam collapsed on the bed when they were gone, not so much in relief as in sorrow.

'They offered me nothing, not even a flower from my own garden. Who are these people?'

'And they think we are like them,' she went on. 'You know, she insisted on paying for the local calls they made; she even wanted to show me the exact number of minutes they spoke! But if she was so bloody meticulous, what about all those calls to New York and Cambridge and places? I can't understand them. Who are these people?' Miriam repeated, walking about the room in consternation, and then suddenly burst into anger, 'I feel violated,' she said. 'They had all the rights and I had all the obligations.'

Mohan smiled wanly. 'That, my love, is American imperialism.'

Ishwar

They first met Ishwar at New Delhi airport the day they arrived in India. Their flight had been delayed, their luggage mislaid and all their attempts to get to the Information Desk were foiled by milling crowds all around them. In desperation, Angela turned to the only man who seemed removed from it all, leaning against a pillar and reading an English newspaper, an unlit cheroot in his mouth.

'Excuse me,' she began tentatively, 'but do you know what time these other offices open?'

The man looked up from his paper. 'H'm. What time?' He scratched his nose. 'That's a good question. It's festival time, you see. Why, what's the problem?'

'It's our luggage, it hasn't arrived, and we haven't booked into a hotel and...'

'OK. Let's see what we can do. Give me your tickets.' He took the tickets from Ronnie, leafed through them and, without ceremony, walked straight into the information office through the staff entrance.

'Why did you give him the tickets like that instead of going with him?' Angela was irritated. 'God knows what —'

'All right, all right. I'll go and stand by the door.' But before Ronnie could move, the man was back.

'Where do you think you'll be staying?' he asked.

'Don't know,' replied Angela.

'You don't want any cheap hotels here – if you have the money?' He looked inquiringly at the couple. 'Especially if you are on your own. Not with a company, are you?'

'No, no, we are on our own,' confirmed Angela. 'But if you can suggest a hotel?'

'Leave it to me,' the man said and disappeared into the office.

'Go on,' Angela urged Ronnie, 'go with him.' But her husband refused to budge and sat himself down by the pillar.

'You go if you want,' he muttered. 'I trust him.'

'He does look educated, I'll give you that,' conceded Angela.

Ten minutes later, the man returned and gave them back their tickets.

'You had better book into the Oberoi,' he advised. 'That's where I told them you are staying. That way you'll get your luggage quicker.'

'That's fine,' said Ronnie. 'Thank you very much. My name is Ronnie and this is my wife Angela. Would you care to have a cup of coffee with us?'

'Ishwar,' the man said, touching his hat. 'I would love a coffee, but I am meeting a friend of mine shortly.' He rummaged in the pockets of his creased tussore suit and came up with a visiting card. 'This is where you'll find me, if you are ever in Calcutta. I do some work for the Tourist Board there.' He offered the card to Angela and, seeing her hesitate, he added laughingly, 'Oh, don't worry. It's just a national habit. Everybody in India has a visiting card.'

'That's very kind of you,' Angela recovered, taking the card from him. 'But we have no plans, really. We thought we'll go as the spirit takes us. Yes?'

'Absolutely,' replied Ishwar. 'That's the only way you'll get to know India. Good luck,' and he shook their hands and left.

Angela was reassured. If it had been up to her, she would have planned the whole trip from beginning to end, or even gone on a package tour, but her father was convinced that the only way to see India was to strike out on their own – and he was paying for the holiday.

'India is an experience,' he had declared with the authority of a man who had spent the most formative years of his life in the Indian Civil Service. 'It means different things to different people. That's why it's no good going with these touristy companies; they make India the same thing for everyone.' And when Angela hesitated, 'Go on, girl, be adventurous for once,' he urged her. 'Try seeing a bit of North India first, and if it works out ... Go on, do it for your dad.'

Angela looked inquiringly at Ronnie.

'I'm all for it,' he said, 'and so will you be, once you get used to the idea.' Ronnie did not quite believe that Angela would, but he went along with the old man because he saw in his persistence a desperate attempt to keep their marriage from breaking up.

Not that Sir Cedric had ever quite approved of Ronnie's marriage to his daughter, partly because he had come to depend on her after his wife had died, and partly because he did not think an accountant was the best match for Angela. She was already too competent for his comfort. A certain efficiency the old man welcomed, it was what kept his life running so smoothly, but Angela carried it into her personal relationships as well. She was always weighing up her friends: who was useful and for what, which friend for a party and which for the opera, and the opera rather than the concert, because the music had a purpose, told a tale. It disconcerted the old man, this trait of his daughter's, and they had quarrelled long and hard over it. He had even accused her of working out her emotions on a balance sheet – and here she was, the branch manager of a high-street bank, going to marry a chartered accountant.

But under the pin-striped suit and the straight back, which were the visible signs of his professional standing, Ronnie hid a persona that craved the abandon that his upbringing had denied him. And Angela somehow moved him to excess. Whether it was her voluptuous beauty or her innocence of it, he was not sure, but together they drove him into a frenzy of desire.

'God, I could die for you,' he burst out when he first set eyes on her at the bar of the golf club.

Angela looked him up and down with her large brooding eyes and said flatly, 'Pardon?'

'I mean, is someone waiting for you? No, no,' he laughed uneasily, 'I mean, are you waiting for someone?'

'Yes, for my father. Cedric Lambton-Smith.'

'Sir Cedric? Ah, he is out there playing with my

boss. Si Battersby? But they won't be finished for some time yet.'

'Oh? Will you give him a message? You'll be here for a while, I expect.' She looked at the glass in his hand.

Ronnie went red. 'Ye-s,' he dragged out.

'Well, tell him I'll pick him up in half an hour, will you?' She turned to go and then looked back at Ronnie. 'Do you play?' she asked.

'Yes, no, I mean sometimes,' stammered Ronnie.

'I'll see you around, then.'

Cold bitch, thought Ronnie, after she had gone, wouldn't even ask my name, but Lord, what a figure – and Ronnie promptly took up golf again, only to discover that Angela did not play golf at all. She merely turned up at the Club to pick up her father on the occasional Friday evening when she had been working late.

It was on one such Friday, when he had just finished his round of golf with Battersby Jnr that Ronnie bumped into Angela again, in the car park. This time he played it cool, inquiring after her and her work, and refusing her invitation to a drink on the ground that he was in training.

'You should play, you know,' he said and, when she replied that she did not know how and her father hadn't the patience to teach her, he had offered to do so. Angela had agreed and, in the course of her lessons, she had thawed towards Ronnie. They had even gone out a few times to the cinema (Ronnie was a film person) and the opera, and kissed and held hands. But at the prospect of anything more intimate, Angela quickly drew back.

Ronnie could not understand it. It was not as if she was cold. On the contrary. She was warm and affectionate and full of laughter. But she kept her body in leash, as though she was afraid that, the moment she let go, it would run away with her. Perhaps it was a reaction to her father's rumbustious life-style. Sir Cedric had been a devoted husband and father, but after his wife died tragically in a car crash (he was driving at the time), he fell back on the bachelor life he had lived in India. Angela was in Oxford then and saw little of her father but, when she finally returned home to London and found him lost and rudderless, she took it upon herself to care for him and organize his life. He still had an eye for the ladies, though, and a tendency to drink himself into forgetfulness — among friends, naturally, and at home mostly, but always to Angela's chagrin. 'Bloody boring business, being a Permanent Secretary,' was how he would justify himself to his daughter, 'I need to —'

'Yes, dad, I know, but it is a responsible business too,' Angela would break in. And the old man would be on his best behaviour for a while.

Slowly, though, Angela was beginning to hate her father's parties and the human mess they created and, after every such occasion, longed even more for privacy and space and order.

Ronnie knew this about her, but had thought that things would be different once they married and set up their own home. Removed from the constraints of looking after her father, she would be able to let herself go, find release for all that passion within her. It only needed him to release it, and the right *ambiance* of course.

The move to the country did indeed change Angela. She loved the quietude of her home and the long strip of garden at the rear which, falling steeply away from the back porch, slipped unobtrusively past its wire-fenced boundary into the fields beyond and over the undulating hills of Hertfordshire, to disappear into the mists and clouds on the horizon. It was a view that took her breath away and made her take up painting.

Yet towards Ronnie she remained the same – loving and attentive and dutiful. She never refused him anything, not even herself, even when she did not feel like making love, but she could never lose herself in him. Even on those rare occasions when they came together, she remained apart, conscious of what was going on, conscious of their coming even, but outside it still. And it left Ronnie outside her, left him feeling that he was ravishing her without her knowledge, enjoying her with no return for her.

The more he gave himself up to her, the more she felt wanting and resentful, and soon she began to blame him for being too demanding. She became snappy and irritable and gave up painting. She went back to golf, hoping to find companionship with Ronnie there, and in the intellectual discussions that they still enjoyed.

But Ronnie now needed more. He hated his job and disliked the Club. He had discovered through Angela that he had to give himself up to something, to someone: a cause, a person, a weakness even. There was an abandon in him that he had never known he possessed till Angela blunted it. His parents had sent him off to boarding-school, though they could ill afford it, because 'the boy was too emotional' and, what was worse, showed it. It was not the type of behaviour that was expected of a career army officer's son, and certainly not if he was going to follow in his father's footsteps, and his grandfather's before him. Luckily for Ronnie, his father died before he had finished school and his mother let him go into accountancy. By then, however, his emotions had been packed away in some dark recess of his psyche.

Till Angela had dredged them up. Ronnie could not believe that he could fall in love with anyone so completely, so naturally. His emotions had found a home in her and he was at ease with himself again. She, in turn, had given herself freely to him, until that last when she had held herself back.

But there was no going back for Ronnie. He had known what it was to lose one's self in someone, and he was not going to lose that again – only now, he had no one to be lost in. He took to drink instead and got lost in himself. And slowly, his marriage began to break up.

That was when old Cedric had stepped in and suggested that they go on holiday to some far distant place and take a long look at themselves. Angela had balked at the idea at first. She had always thought that married couples should get away from each other from time to time to keep their marriage fresh, not take the same old marriage to some new place in the hope of renewing it. If a marriage was finished, it was finished, and no amount of relocating it was going to bring it back. Ronnie had gone along with her: not once, in all their five years of marriage, had they been on holiday together. Well, this time, she told her father, she would give it a try; it would probably be the first and last time.

India, though, was not her idea of a holiday place. It was too noisy and crowded for that, and they needed peace and quiet to work out their differences. Cedric was adamant: a completely foreign experience would be good for them; and, in the same vein, he had suggested that they should not plan their itinerary but go from place to place as their fancy, and money, took them.

And that was what they had set out to do, with only a guidebook as companion. But losing their luggage on arrival had not been the most auspicious of beginnings – and staying at the Oberoi had tempted them into falling in with the tours that the hotel arranged for its guests. In the first three days alone, they had done the Red Fort, 'the symbol of Moghul power', the Jami Masjid, 'the largest mosque in India', the ruins of Ferozabad at Feroz Shah Kotla 'with its 13-metre high sandstone pillar of Ashoka inscribed with his edicts', the Lutyens Parliament buildings (twice) and innumerable museums, tombs and mausoleums. The trip to the Taj Mahal was scheduled for the following week.

'We have become typical tourists,' said Angela at breakfast, on the fourth day of their stay. 'Exactly what father did not want us to do.'

'You are right,' replied Ronnie, 'let's go to Agra on our own. Just jump into the train and go. Ask around for a decent hotel and see the Taj.'

'And from there to Fatehpur Sikri?' Angela was look-ing at the guidebook that she had taken out of her handbag as Ronnie was speaking. 'That is the city that the great emperor Akbar built in 1570, it says here. Forty kilometres from Agra.'

'Agreed.'

'When, then?'

'Day after tomorrow? I'd like to get over all this rapid-fire sight-seeing business of the last few days and get a feel of the place.'

'Fine. I'll laze around the pool and do a round of the shops before we strike out into the wilderness.'

'Strike out into the wilderness?'

'Before I fortify myself for the train journey, then,' giggled Angela.

No amount of preparation, however, could help her come to terms with the journey itself. There were people everywhere, on the train and in the train, above and below and beside her, separating her from Ronnie and threatening to separate her from herself. Everyone was considerate towards her, though, and when the train finally began to move, she found herself being ac-commodated on a cool tin trunk and attended to by an old lady who fanned Angela's face with the end piece of her sari. Still, she was relieved when they got off at Agra.

'Look at me,' she said, tugging at her blouse, 'I am soaked right through. I don't want another trip like that ever again.'

'I am sorry,' apologized Ronnie, 'we'll reserve our seats beforehand next time. First class.' His shirt was torn and his lanky frame looked as though it had been put through a lathe. Angela's face broke into a reluctant smile.

'The people were nice, anyway, and I did have a re-served seat after all, and air-conditioning of sorts.' She took Ronnie's arm. 'Come on, let's find a quiet hotel and rest up for a day or two.'

But she was up at daybreak the following morning and, gathering up Ronnie, set out for the Taj Mahal. There were few visitors at that time of day, and they were able to take in the monument at their own pace. Angela had waited a long time for this moment and, like a votary going up to receive communion, she walked slowly through the walled gardens and ambled along the water course before standing before the great dome. And she marvelled at the sheer symmetry of it all: the eloquence of its mathematical precision and the silence of its monumental stillness.

She gathered up her long auburn hair in a knot. 'I must come here again,' she said reflectively. 'At sunset.'

The next day, however, Angela decided to hire a taxi and go to Fatehpur Sikri instead. By the time they returned from the trip, it was too late to visit the Taj Mahal. Besides, Angela wanted to put down her impres-sions of Fatehpur Sikri in her notebook while they were still fresh in her mind, and she had to write to her father.

'What's one evening, anyway?' she said, more to her-self than to Ronnie. 'We own our time.'

Ronnie was startled. 'Oh, I say, you are not letting yourself go, are you? What's next, I wonder.'

'What's next,' declared Angela, returning to her best sergeant-major manner, 'is the Taj Mahal. Tomorrow evening. That's the best time, I'm told.'

But the Taj Mahal at sunset, Angela discovered, was no more beautiful or awe-inspiring than at any other time of day. She was affected, though, by the play of moonlight on marble and the eerie sense of loneliness and longing it evoked in her.

'Brr,' she growled, shaking off the ghostly feeling and sitting down beside Ronnie on the steps to the entrance. 'It's as still as a tomb.'

'And as cold as the grave,' Ronnie came back, rising to what he took to be his wife's witticism.

'It is really very splendid, isn't it?'

Ronnie scratched his head. 'Yes, it's an astonishing piece of work, I suppose.'

'Suppose?'

'No, no, I am awed by it all right. But it does not grab me here,' and he held his solar plexus. 'It doesn't move me. Perhaps it's the marble. There's no warmth in marble. It's a cold beauty, and the moonlight makes it colder still.'

'It's a tomb, man,' snapped Angela.

'But, Ange, it's also a hymn to love.'

Angela looked quizzically at her husband. 'The grave's a fine and private place,' she quoted, 'but none, I think, do there embrace.'

'That's exactly what he wanted to do, though, isn't it? Shah Jehan? Embrace his Mumtaz forever, even in the grave? But he turned it into such a fine and private place that we forget the embrace.'

'Now you are trying to be clever,' said Angela.

'No, Ange, it's simply that ... oh, I don't know what I am trying to say.' He took out a bottle of water and, taking a sip from it, handed it to Angela. 'You see, I am moved by it, like you are. But in the head. Of course, I am touched by the sheer beauty of it, to the point of being hurt, but it's only when I am told the story of their love that it begins to touch my heart.'

Angela did not quite understand what Ronnie was driving at, but she didn't think he did either.

'H'm, all right,' she conceded after a while, 'but what about Fatehpur Sikri, then? Would you say that that is over-elaborate too?'

'Funny you should say that. That was what I thought at first. But then it's a whole city, isn't it — the palace, the mosque, the cloisters, the harem? Fashioned out of a particular social order, and reflecting it?'

'So?'

'It's all of a piece. The lay-out, the architecture, the design, they are all of a piece, whole, with a purpose, and yet, and yet ... not quite organic.'

Angela looked at her husband. In the moonlight, his face seemed softer, more thoughtful.

'This is becoming a bit of a thing with you, isn't it. This organic?'

Ronnie smiled self-consciously. 'Oh, I don't know, Ange. But recently I have been thinking that we accountants are very good at seeing bits and pieces, but never the whole.'

'And? There is an and somewhere, isn't there?'

'And it seems to make us bits and pieces, too. Mechanical.'

'Or we were like that in the first place to have been attracted to the job?' Angela suggested.

Ronnie put his arms around her and drew her closer to him, noticing how the moonlight burnished her hair. 'Where to next, O great leader?' he asked, helping her to her feet.

'I thought you wanted to go to Khajuraho, you dirty bugger, and from there to Bombay or Calcutta. You choose. They are either side of Khajuraho.'

'Calcutta, then.'

'But from now on, we are flying,' insisted Angela, 'even if there are stop-overs. I have had enough of trains and crowds.'

'Well, India is crowds,' muttered Ronnie under his breath – and more so on festival days, he might have added, as they discovered when they arrived in Khajuraho. Angela, however, was not interested in taking a closer look at sculpted lovers on the temple walls and was content to view them from a distance. It was not her scene, she told Ronnie, though he kept pointing out that the women were as ample and beautiful as her – if more giving, he added *sotto voce*.

'Just look at it, Ange,' he enthused. 'The Kama Sutra played out in stone on God's house.' He threw up his arms and shouted, 'I want to become a Hindu.'

'What, just to fuck yourself silly?'

'No, it's not just that. The Hindus accept life in its totality, its beauty, filth and all, celebrate life in its totality. Procreation, death, lust, love, the lot. Whereas us Christians or even the Muslims...'

'What about the Muslims?'

'I don't know, but look at all that Mogul stuff – the mosques and the minarets and the ... all breathtakingly beautiful, but cold, removed, aloof – and their cities, so neat and functional. And their God, too, is removed, above, peerless and alone.' They had moved closer to the largest temple as they were speaking, and they now sat down on the ground before it. 'But for the Hindus,' Ronnie went on, 'why, their Gods are everywhere, in the soul, in the flesh, in the lingam and the yoni, as prone to sin and salvation as you or me.'

'OK, OK,' laughed Angela. 'You have made your case. You have my permission to become a Hindu.' She stood up and beat the dust from her dress with her hat. 'In which case, I had better take you to Benares, or Varanasi as you Hindus say, and baptize you in the Ganges.'

Ronnie was grateful to Angela for suggesting it; a dip in the holy river was something to look forward to. But, when she got him to Varanasi and stood him before the Ganges, Ronnie began to lose his enthusiasm. The steps leading to the river ran for miles along it, yet there was not one spot they could see which did not overflow with people – bathing, washing, praying, meditating, begging – alongside cows, monkeys, goats, dogs, cats and crows. While the water, murky and dirty with myriad burnt offerings floating atop of it, barely flowed. Ronnie put his foot in and quickly drew it out again.

'So Hinduism is also dirt and filth and floating faeces,' Angela commented dryly.

'Maybe,' Ronnie gave in reluctantly, 'but see how they value their personal cleanliness.'

'Letting others clean up their mess, you mean,' retaliated Angela. 'No wonder they need to have castes.'

'What has that got to do with anything?' protested Ronnie. 'In any case, you've got to see it in the round. Hinduism is not just a religion or a philosophy but a whole social system.' He went on to expound boringly and at length on what Angela derided as his latest addiction, and ended by asserting that she would have a different view of things when they went the round of the temples in the morning.

Angela, though, refused to go with him and, left to his own enthusiasms, Ronnie went from temple to shrine, enjoying the hustle and bustle of Hindu worship and the mysterious intonings of the priests at *pooja*. It was only when he set off for Calcutta with Angela the following day that he realized that he had been robbed of his wallet and traveller's cheques – and his headlong affair with Hinduism became touched with disillusion.

Angela took the whole episode rather more stoically: the tickets at least were in her custody, and she had expected Ronnie's 'abandon' to land him in a hole sooner or later. But, when they arrived at Calcutta airport, she was visited again by that dread sense of being out of control that had gripped her, on and off, like a vice in her journey through India.

'What are we going to do now?' she moaned. 'We can phone father and reverse the charges, and we'll have just enough money left for a cheap hotel for the night.'

'Where?' asked Ronnie.

Angela took out her guidebook and leafed through it.

'I know,' said Ronnie, brightening up. 'We can ring that guy, what's his name? Ishwar? You have got his card, haven't you?'

'I don't know. Whoever thought we'd land up in Calcutta, let alone want to see Ishwar?' She searched for the card in her handbag.

'Ah, here it is,' she exclaimed in triumph, handing the card over to Ronnie and then, more dejectedly, 'but who knows where he'll be.'

Luckily for them, Ishwar was at home and, what was more, remembered Angela and Ronnie.

'How could I forget?' he laughed. 'Your wife was afraid to take my card.'

Ronnie apologized profusely and went on to tell Ishwar about their predicament. Could Ishwar tell them where they could find cheap, suitable accommodation?

'Leave it to me,' said Ishwar in characteristic fashion, and gave Ronnie an address to go to.

'It's more a hostel than a hotel, but it's comfortable and cheap and I'll meet you there. It's close to my place and I shall probably be there before you.'

Ishwar hadn't arrived by the time Angela and Ronnie got to the hostel. They hung around on the veranda for a while and then went in search of the tearoom to find a comfortable seat and get something to eat. They had been travelling all day, and the last bit of the journey from the airport, being driven through the streets and alleyways of Calcutta in an auto-rickshaw that dodged its way in and out of traffic, cows, crowds and sundry obstacles, with their baggage threatening to escape them at every turn and twist, had brought Angela to the point of exhaustion. All she wanted now was to eat something and fall into bed. But the restaurant, such as it was, was deserted. There were no customers or waiters about, although it was only ten at night. Ronnie went up to the reception clerk and persuaded him to open the tea-room and fetch them some tea and sandwiches. What they got, instead, was coffee and Indian sweetmeats – and that, half an hour later.

'Christ, how on earth did we end up here?' cried Angela. 'It's all your damn fault.' She whisked away the flies from the plate of sweetmeats angrily, but they were back the next minute. 'Cover the damn thing with that other plate, will you?'

'What, and eat the plates?' retorted Ronnie illogically.

Just then, Ishwar arrived and, seeing Angela desperately driving the flies away, signalled to the clerk to fetch a wire net to cover the plate. 'All you have to do now,' he smiled, 'is to lift the cover to take what you want, and your fly problem is solved.' He shook hands with Angela and Ronnie and welcomed them to Calcutta.

'I see you haven't had a proper meal,' he observed. 'You must be starving.'

'But the restaurant is closed,' Angela pointed out.

'Leave it to me,' said Ishwar, calling the clerk over and ordering chapattis and chicken curry. 'At midnight, he also becomes a waiter,' he explained, 'a sort of Indian Cinderella.'

When the food was served and the waiter had turned clerk again, Ishwar went up to the desk to arrange their accommodation.

'He is such a calming influence, isn't he?' Angela remarked, beginning to unwind. 'I wonder how he does it.'

'Here he is. Ask him,' said Ronnie, and then went on to ask the question himself.

'Years of practice,' laughed Ishwar. 'Years of practice.' He gave Angela the key to their room. 'It's the best room in the hostel, you know, with its own shower and toilet. Oh yes, and a balcony. Overlooking the main street, though.'

He sat down and watched the couple finish their supper. 'OK?' he asked. They nodded eagerly, swallowing the last mouthful. Ishwar looked at his watch. 'You should go to bed,' he said, 'and so should I.' He rose to go. 'I have told the clerk to put a mosquito net over your bed, not that you'll want it in this heat.'

Angela looked at Ronnie. They had scraped each other's nerves raw these last few days, and the thought of sharing a bed did not appeal to her. She wanted room to breathe.

'Thank you, Ishwar.' Ronnie rose from the table. 'If not for you —'

'Yes, without you we would have been completely lost,' Angela interjected.

'Oh, please, it's nothing. I'll see you tomorrow. Around evening? It's Sunday and you need the rest. Sleep well.'

'We'll try,' laughed Angela, putting a bold face on

her apprehensions. The room, though, was large and airy and the bed comfortable and, exhausted, they fell asleep as soon as they lay down.

Angela woke up at noon the following day, rang her father for money and tried to go back to sleep again. But she had now become conscious of Ronnie's snoring and the noises outside and, picking up a book, she went on to the balcony. The street below was crowded and teeming with life even though it was a Sunday, but Angela did not mind that at this distance. In fact, she tried to look at it the way she thought Ishwar might and began at last to accept that India was a country of contradictions. She said as much to Ishwar at dinner that evening.

Ishwar was not sure whether contradiction was the right word. 'I would say paradox,' he said thoughtfully. 'India is full of paradoxes, not contradictions.'

'What's the difference?' asked Ronnie.

'A contradiction is capable of resolution, but a paradox by definition ... Or, put it this way, you can resolve a contradiction, but you've got to live with a paradox.'

Angela was fascinated. 'Go on, please,' she urged Ishwar.

'A contradiction is when two truths vie with each other.' Ishwar's eyes sparkled with discovery. 'In a paradox they coexist. India is backward and progressive, traditional and modern, feudal and capitalist. Nothing dies here, everything coexists, side by side.'

Angela mulled over the idea for a while but found it hard to accept. She pushed the plate away from her and leant across the table. 'But what does all that mean in real life?' she challenged Ishwar. 'How does it apply to ordinary people? How can they coexist if they are swarming all over each other? Where's the space?'

Ishwar bristled. 'Space, space. You people go on about space and privacy as though you need to have space to have a relationship. But it is the relationship that creates space. You can belong to someone and yet be private. To give up your freedom to another and have it returned to you — that is space.' He finished with a flourish and guffawed. 'At this rate I'll be taking myself seriously,' he said.

'Don't put yourself down,' admonished Angela, liking him the more for his self-deprecation. 'I've understood more about your country in the last five minutes than from all the books I've read.'

'What about the Hindu-Muslim conflict, then?' Ronnie was off on his own quest.

'A political expedient, not a social construct,' declared Ishwar, now comfortably into his stride.

'Not religious, either?' inquired Ronnie.

'No,' replied Ishwar and they fell to talking about religion. Angela lost interest at that point and, excusing herself, went up to bed.

She could not sleep. Ishwar's words rang in her ears, and the experiences of the past weeks were shaping themselves into a kaleidoscope of patterns and meanings — and she was uncomfortable. She got up from bed and walked on to the balcony. The street was less busy and less noisy. She pulled up a chair and sat down, watching the people go by.

Suddenly, a movement across the street catches her eye. A man is making his bed for the night on the pavement by the sewer. (Making his bed, what an absurd expression, she thinks, from another time, another place, when what he is doing is spreading layers of cardboard on the ground.) His three children are already asleep beside him and his wife, after covering them from the night with newspapers from the street, makes her nightly ablutions from a tin of water before stretching herself out beside her mother on the other side. A mangy dog curls up at their feet, and the jasmine tree in the grounds of the great house behind their bit of pavement flowers over them.

Angela crept back into bed and waited for Ronnie.

Celia

He wondered why Celia wanted to see him. It was years since she had set out with any definite purpose to visit him – not since she had got married, anyway. Was she looking for a job? But then why the urgency, barely concealed beneath the flat monotone of her unemotive upper-class voice? It was the most unattractive voice he had known. It grated and rasped even as it whined, quasi-nasal, always on the same note, sans brio, sans sorrow, electric with breeding and the authority of riches.

The door of his room was open and she came in. He rose from his chair to meet her, all memory of her voice forgotten in the excitement of seeing again the Della Robbia face on the Reubens body. And the eyes – they were innocent still and wide with wonderment compounded of expectation. But they took in his assistants in the bookshop before coming back to him, and he knew he must be restrained.

The shop was shut now, and he returned to his room. She was looking at the display shelves with her back to him. He went up to her and put his hand across her shoulder. She turned and came into him, her mouth slightly open, her eyes all anticipation. They kissed, long and desperately, with different desperations: he with the abiding memory of a time when, seized with an ague of love, he had poured it all into her one evening, only to find her drained even of herself — and she? He did not know, as yet, but was keened to a sense of self-immolation.

They undressed in the half light that broke in through the window, she so casual and he throbbing once again with virgin excitement — it could have been a hundred times before but it was always new to him. And now, with her, it was the very first time, and more, something continued without a sense of break after two long years. He paused to look at her breasts and moved towards her to help her out of her brassiere, wanting to touch the sheer roundnesses of her, quickly, urgently, before they fell from the cups of her bra into an amorphous mass.

But, oh, they held, they stood, rounder than ever and firm, rotund, moon-faced, full to bursting and tender-hard like a phallus. The bra was a convention.

He lingered over her breasts, suckled at them till their stalks were as erect as him, and proud and round and safe. Loath to move away from them, and yet trembling with the desire to discover her other roundnesses, he unzipped her skirt at the back, sensing already beneath her briefs the globularity of her buttocks. Such perfect cheeks, orbs of sheer perfection, but lengthening as she moved, into eccentric circles, a very paradox of roundness.

And her crotch was like her face, innocent and bright and expectant, sweet smelling under her bush of gold. He ached with the fervour of seed unshed.

'Raymond and I still love each other,' she rasped, paused, 'You are the first man ... He and I don't hit it off sexually ... He thinks I should see a psychiatrist ... But I am not sure that it's not him...'

To cover all that glory, in front and behind, he was thinking, how could one man hope to envelop it all, bring all this roundness to the point of a single ecstasy ... when her voice broke in on him.

'Raymond wouldn't mind ... He has other women and I must know whether it's me ... Oh I am sorry. I didn't mean to upset you.'

His erection was gone from him, the seed had lapsed, the unending roundness of his George Keyt world ceased and became angular, spiky, unsafe. He was slivered.

And he was sad, for her, standing there so uncaring of her body, unaware, unloving of herself, inglorious. Somewhere on the road which led from her imperial past to the portals of the LSE and her South African sculptor husband, she had found that she had mislaid the centre of her being. Her education had told her that much, as had that other world that penetrated through to her from her African friends. But she could not find it, and did not know how.

He must try, he must come erect again, he wanted it so much for her, she must be released, if he failed her now...

He failed.

'I am sorry,' he said, putting on his trousers, and then, more bitterly, 'the stereotype doesn't work. Some of us natives aren't simply functional.'

'No, it isn't like that. I have loved you for so long. I respect you, you were the only one who could tell me, show me … who I am, was. Do you know what I mean? It's something about our civilization — the life-force has been drained out of us. Somehow we look to you whom we have despised as wogs and niggers and savages to save us from ourselves. But that is to savage you all over again, isn't it?'

For the first time since he had known her, she was close to real despair, real understanding, a whole caring for someone else. The moment passed. He was alone.

A Long Day's Journey

'Oh, hello Anna, you've got here at last. Dick —'

'Yes, where is Dick? This is Nanda.'

'He is not very well you know. Hello Mr Nanda. Shouldn't be here. Nice to meet you. It's the gall bladder. He is in the bar, taking his tablets. Yes it is the old trouble I think. You remember he had a pain in his stomach sometime ago, and the doctors, they are useless, they said, you don't mind, Mr Nanda, do you, they said that it was nothing and come in for observation. Middlesex Hospital has been observing him, now he gets a temperature as well, never mind, that's only the first bell. So, how are you Anna, but you can't trust doctors these days. They gave him some tablets and it is not his gall bladder they say, nothing wrong with him, then why do they give him tablets? I wanted him to stay at home, but he wouldn't hear of it. No, no, he was not being polite, he wants to see the play himself. You know what he is like when it comes to plays, and the Old Vic besides. We were at the Mermaid last week and we have got tickets for Sadler's Wells on Thursday — it's too much you think? Well Aunty Gerda is looking after the children. You know Aunty Gerda, Mr Nanda? Oh, yes, Anna must have told you. They are still on their holidays but it's not too bad this time. Dick and I

have got about a bit, they are no trouble to Aunty
Gerda. Of course Dick will do everything. You know
him, he will be angry that I have told you. So don't say
anything. I mean don't make a fuss or anything. You
know how he is, oh it doesn't matter, that is only the
second bell – no, no, there is one more, I am sure. Yes,
yes, one more. So I'll tell you quickly, we never have
time for a real conversation. Every time I meet you or
you come home, you are in a hurry. This temperature,
you see, keeps coming back, it is not good I tell you,
today he came home at 3.30, most unusual. So how was
Vienna? We are going soon, it is so expensive now, are
there any porters? This friend, you know Mrs Levy,
don't you? Eighty-two, oh yes, eighty-two, over if anything. She had all these bags coming from Los Angeles
and going to Paris, Rome, Berlin, Istanbul and all those
places, and there were no porters, not one, not at
Victoria, nor Folkestone, not even at Calais, let alone
Rome – terrible. So she took this huge trolley, eighty-
two, I tell you, she took this trolley and put all her bags
in it and rolled it to the train, right up to the train. You
must get on the waiting lists for everything these days,
Mr Nanda, even porters. Oh yes, talking about waiting
lists, they got a useful mailing system now at the Old
Vic, free, so you know in advance what is on, no queu-
ing for tickets or anything, you don't even have to wait
till the programmes are published in the paper, they
send you notices of all the plays they are putting on,
and you get your tickets, cheap seats too, by mail, and
you can make arrangements for the children and do all
your chores and things, no waste of time or anything

and so we are able to come early and watch the people, we know lots of their faces now. Anna tells me you are a teacher, Mr Nanda. That's how we were here before you though you live close by, and the people ... hello there is no one about, good heavens, I could have sworn there was another bell. Or is that at the Aldwych? Come come ... Dick? Where's Dick? Ah, here you are ... What do you mean we can't go to our seats till the interval, oh, end of first scene, but the first scene is so long, best part of the play, oh well ... we'll stand here at the back then.'

Nanda had not been to the theatre for three years: he could not plan plays and concerts, plan his receptiveness, beforehand. O'Neill, though, had been his dark companion in the days of his own family break-up and, wishing now to view the man's darkness from the outside, he had gathered up his receptiveness and was expectant, had been for days, ever since he was invited to a *Long Day's Journey* by these friends of Anna. He was even prepared to masquerade as her lover, though the affair was now long over. And here he was, with the whole of the first scene well-nigh gone – or, perhaps, it had been played out in the foyer.

He glanced resentfully at Leoni, standing in front and to the side of him, to find that she was already switched on to the play. The frivolity was gone from her face and a brooding melancholy was clouding it over. The transformation was so sudden that Nanda could not help but think that it had been prepared earlier and made ready for the occasion. It had already been intimated in talk of gall bladders, mysterious spasms, sudden sickness and tablets taken secretly, but modestly, under cover of the crowd in the bar. And, of course, she had read the text before coming. Perhaps it was all part of the professional theatre-goer's equipment, a sort of *vade-mecum* – a stock of emotions carefully garnered and kept and trained to come out at the right moment in response to the right stimulus. With O'Neill, it was dark despair and lengthy speeches. But what if it was Becket or Pinter? Would her monologue be reduced to a sentence? Would she be wearing sackcloth and ashes? Nanda smiled to himself as he ran his eyes over her mourning-black gown. She was a tall, imposing woman with a banked-up, middle-age, middle-European sexuality in her somewhere. Perhaps she could still waken to Albee, be carried along by the current of his sexual traumas and, furtively, under cover of the half-light, place a fervid hand on her husband's thigh. And how would Dick respond, wondered Nanda, squinting at the figure standing lean and hunched and English beside her. Would he...? No, he was a Noel Coward man, light and frothy and inconsequential. Nanda chuckled silently; he was beginning to enjoy his own little play. Served them right for messing up his evening.

'So, what are you writing now?' Leoni asked, as they spilled out into the foyer at the interval. 'I have just started your short stories. Anna gave –'

'Oh? Did she?' Nanda stammered, 'I hope you –'

'I am sure I'll like them. I was telling Dick ... Where's Dick?' She looked over the heads of the crowd. 'Must have gone to the toilet.' She put her handkerchief to her nose. 'Prostate,' she bent down and whispered in Nanda's ear. 'I think I'll join him,' she giggled.

Nanda lifted his eyes to heaven, but Anna took no notice. 'Where on earth did you pick her up?' he asked in desperation.

'Don't be so cruel. Leoni and her family lost everything in the Holocaust.' She paused. 'What am I saying? She has no family to speak of. My mother is her only family, and Aunty Gerda. They were distant cousins but went to the same school for a while, my mother and Leoni, I mean. Aunty Gerda was Leoni's nanny, they all call her Aunty Gerda. Leoni's father was a famous surgeon but was hounded out by the Nazis in 1939. She must have been seventeen at the time. Do you know that Leoni and her sister had private tutors and had their own box at the Staatsoper and the Salzburg Festival Theatre?' Anna was indignant. 'Their lives revolved around the arts. And it was all taken from them. Like that.' She snapped her fingers. 'You should see the bits of silverware in Leoni's house even today.' Anna went on, hoping to awe Nanda into submission, 'All monogrammed —'

'What happened to her sister?' interrupted Nanda.

'What? Oh, her? She married Mrs Levy's son. Runs a chain of jewellery shops in Bogota.'

'So that's the Levy that Leoni was referring to,' Nanda murmured. 'Levy the traveller through the diaspora, looking for porters.'

'Sorry, I didn't get that.'

'Never mind. And what happened to Aunty Gerda?'

'She got caught smuggling food and was put in a

concentration camp – Auschwitz I think – but she managed to survive and escaped to England somehow.'

'So all the rich Jews got away with all their chattels to various parts of the world while the poor Jews became fodder for the gas chambers?' Nanda commented. 'And those who survived are servants once more to the rich Jews or end up in Israel as fodder for Zion?'

'That's rubbish,' Anna bristled. 'Leoni has nothing. Her sister, yes. My mother says she even took her grand piano with her. But Leoni, no. She has nothing except her memories and mementoes and her trips to the theatre. Dick was an unemployed architect when she first met him, does not have much work even now, and they had to start life all over again, like my parents. My mother ran a boarding...' She broke off as she saw Leoni and Dick approaching. 'We'll take this up later,' she bit out under her breath.

Nanda realized that he had upset Anna and put out a mollifying hand to her during the performance, but she was unyielding. The whole evening was spoilt for him now and he could not wait for the play to be over. Some of his old feeling for Anna was returning. He had liked the way she had stood up for Leoni. It reminded him of the time when he was going through a messy divorce and she alone, of all his friends, had refused to believe the monstrous stories of cruelty that his wife was putting around. Anna had stood up for him then, and cared for him, and he had thought that she would always be there. Taken her for granted, perhaps. Or too demanding, maybe. It had all happened too soon after his break-up with Mala: the recriminations had left him emptied of love, and the frenzy with which he threw himself into his affair with Anna seemed to have exhausted her. You hold me too close, she had said, and left him.

'How about a drink?' he whispered to Anna, as they were leaving the theatre. 'Just us two.' But before Anna could reply, Leoni called out from behind them that Dick was going to treat them to coffee and cake at the new Continental Café round the corner.

Nanda kept on walking, but Anna pulled him back. 'Oh come on, don't let's spoil her evening just because she spoilt ours,' she pleaded, and Nanda gave in.

'Don't worry, Mr Nanda,' Leoni placated him, as they sat down to mocha and strudel. 'We won't keep you love-birds long,' and, turning to Anna, she added, 'Aunty Gerda goes to bed at eleven.'

'How is Aunty Gerda?' asked Anna, and suddenly Leoni's face folded back into its creases.

'Dying,' she said softly. 'Her lungs. Gone. And her heart.'

'It was those damp rooms she lived in all those years,' she went on after a while, 'and of course the camp. How much we tried to get her to come and live with us, but she wanted her independence.'

'But I thought she moved in with you —'

'Not till after her second heart attack, and not till Dick had built the extension.' Leoni suppressed a smile.

'Hasn't she got a sister in Israel?'

'Yes, her twin, and she misses her, but will she go? How many times I have told her, if you won't live with us, go and live with your sister. Go to Israel. But she won't have that either. You know why? Because they are not real Jews, she says, only pretendjers and revenjers, she says, in her broken English – pretend Jews and revenge Jews she means, Mr Nanda. They have lost the meaning of suffering, she says in German, and so have lost the meaning of justice.' She shook her head gently from side to side. 'The spirit of that woman. It's what has kept us going, you know.'

John Fortune

Lindiwe was sure she was being followed. By the same man. Not stalked, but followed. Nobody stalked anybody in King's Cross. Or followed anybody, for that matter, except to cadge the price of a drink. Lindiwe was used to that. She had been working at the Centre on Poverty on Caledonian Road for about five years now, and in that time she had seen that part of King's Cross, east of the station, decline from a busy, albeit down-market and small-time, commercial area into a mess of derelict shop-fronts and dark alleyways where drug-pushers plied their trade and prostitutes flaunted their wares. A pub here and a bank there picked up the pennies and the pounds of the black economy, and a bookshop held on like faith for better days to come. But the only auguries for the future were the desultory portakabins that the police set up from time to time to clear the streets for the tourists.

Lindiwe knew most of the street dwellers by sight and would pass them by with a nod and a smile. Anything more familiar was not called for, and assistance of any sort was taboo — from the locals, anyway. The tourists were another matter, and the American hotel at the more respectable end of King's Cross made sure that there was a steady supply of those.

Most of the others at the Centre were afraid to walk to the station alone after dark, but Lindiwe floated along without a fear in the world. This was her patch, her little jungle and she knew it well, knew its dangers and was unafraid. It was no more dangerous than the slums of her native Johannesburg, in which she had grown up and would be living still, but for the grace of God and the Bishop of Soweto, who had got her a scholarship to study abroad. As it was, she had escaped the poverty and misery of apartheid, escaped to England and freedom, but she still looked back over her shoulder at those she felt she had abandoned. And, although she sent money to her parents, living sparingly herself, and her work at the Centre enabled her to channel funds to the townships back home, she could not overcome the sense of guilt she felt at being the fortunate one. She should be there, working on the ground, her ground, the ground she knew so well, not fobbing off the job with grants to well-meaning outsiders who had no feel for the people or their problems. She had thought she could be of use to the denizens of King's Cross, but there was nothing she could do for them: they had gone beyond despair into an underworld of their own.

But this man who followed her, he did not belong here, above ground or below, neither tourist nor denizen. He was too shabbily dressed for the one and too long in the tooth for the other; no one on the street lived long enough to grow that old.

He was sixty, if he was a day, thought Lindiwe, and looked the very image of a dirty old man – tall and stooped, in a crumpled old raincoat and a battered felt

hat, staring short-sightedly at the pimps and the prostitutes from under the faded awning of the bookshop.
That was why Lindiwe had noticed him when she had
gone in to buy a book for her godmother: the stereotype was too flagrant to be missed. She saw him there
the following day, and off and on for the next two
weeks in the run-up to Christmas, at four o'clock of an
evening, when the winter light was fading and Lindiwe
was hurrying home.

Then he disappeared altogether, and Lindiwe had all
but forgotten him when, on a cold February day, she
saw him follow her all the way to the Centre. But,
when she turned round at the door, he had gone. She
did not see him again for a while after that, but, about
two weeks later, she found him following her again, at a
distance at first, but closer and closer as the days went
by – till, one morning, she found him at the door of the
Centre, waiting for it to open.

'What is it you want?' Lindiwe burst out, shocked
out of her usual kindliness, and the man, startled, managed to stammer out, 'I, I . . . Sorry' in a high-pitched
voice before he turned on his heels and fled.

Lindiwe slammed the door behind her and, picking
up the mail, took it into Mr Ahmad's office, to find that
the director had already come in.

'What on earth is the matter, Lindiwe?' asked
Ahmad, as she handed him the post. 'You look angry
and displeased.'

'It's this man, boss,' Lindiwe sank into the visitor's
chair across Ahmad's desk. 'I am sure he is following
me. A shabby old man –'

'Ah, the chap who was hanging around, watching all those people.'

'Oh yes. I told you about him, didn't I? I am sure he means no harm. Not that I am afraid of him or anything.' Her eyes lit up with battle.

'No, I should say not,' laughed Ahmad, looking at Lindiwe's portly figure. 'Your walk alone is enough to frighten anyone.'

'But he's weird. There's something not right there.' Lindiwe lit a cigarette and Ahmad pushed the ashtray towards her. 'There's a, there's a ... what is that saying of yours?'

'Which one?' inquired Ahmad uneasily. Lindiwe was always teasing him about his colonial education and his fondness for proverbs and quotations.

'You know ... when something is not right and you feel it. A sort of out-of-tune thing.'

'A rift in the lute, you mean,' offered Ahmad carefully.

'That is it, a rift in the lute, that is the feeling I get every time I see him. Uneasy, that's what I am, uneasy.' Lindiwe stubbed out her cigarette and rose to go. 'Don't worry, boss, it will pass. Or he will,' she added with a guffaw.

'I have no doubt about that, Lindiwe. There's nothing and no one you cannot handle.'

A week later, Lindiwe came up to Ahmad's desk, all flushed and flustered.

'It's that man again, boss. I could not mistake that squeaky voice of his. On the phone.'

'What man?'

'You know, the old fellow I told you about? Who was following me?'

'Ah, him. On the phone? What does he want?'

'Oh, he wanted to know about the changes in our organization — whether we are still a charity and, if so, how could we bring out such a controversial paper like *Power and Poverty*. Weren't we afraid of being closed down? That sort of thing. Do you want to speak to him?'

'Did he ask for me?' inquired Ahmad, 'I mean, did he want somebody in authority? Is he that type of man?'

'No, he didn't, not really. But he is funny. Wanted to know how we publish things, run a library and hold meetings, all on a staff of three or four. Things like that. I told him we had volunteers, and then he questions that. How do we get them? Why do they volunteer? When I replied that they probably find our work now speaks to their problems, he paused a long while and said, "Oh, I see." Funny man. Could be anything, a nutter or a National Front guy, or someone from the Charity Commission, spying on us after that article in the *Mail*.'

'Well, don't keep him hanging on. Be guarded in what you say and try to find out what he really wants. Why not ask him directly? Or tell him to come and see us. We can assess him better then.'

'Yes, all right, if you say so,' condescended Lindiwe and sashayed out of the room. She came back a few minutes later.

'Did you find out anything more?' Ahmad queried.

'I told you, he is mad. When I asked him about him and what he did, he went off on a long tale about how he was in a similar position as ourselves. I don't know what he means except that he is broke and wants money – wants to give us money, too, but hasn't any. And then he asked for suggestions as to how he could get some "untainted" funds, yes untainted was the word he used, for his own work, work with people he said. He had heard that we had broken with big business and industry and had no money, and yet had managed to survive. "Carry on",' Lindiwe mimicked the man's high nasal tone, '"carry on the good work". I am sure he is a nut, or he has been put up by somebody to check on us.'

'You are beginning to develop a siege mentality,' Ahmad reproached her gently. 'Is he going to come in?'

'Yes, that's the only way I could get rid of him. And you had better see him when he comes. I've had enough...'

On the following Monday, Lindiwe accosted Ahmad in the corridor.

'You just missed him,' she said. 'He was passing this area, he said, and dropped in. I spoke to him at the door – I was going to the bank – and got rid of him quickly. He is coming in next week, though. That man I was telling you about,' she added, as Ahmad looked blankly at her. 'You know, the nut who wanted to know about our Centre, made all those inquiries the other day.'

'Oh yes,' nodded Ahmad, 'that guy. Good. I'll see him when he comes.'

Four days later, Lindiwe stormed into Ahmad's room.

'He is here, he is here,' she said in an agitated whisper, 'that mad man —'

'Show him in,' interrupted Ahmad,

A large shabby man with greying hair and a stoop, ruddy-complexioned, coat and hat in hand, walked in after Lindiwe.

Ahmad looked up from his desk and rose quickly from his chair with both arms outstretched, ignoring Lindiwe's clandestine warnings to be discreet.

'Reverend John Fortune,' he greeted the man, 'how nice to see you. Please sit down.'

Lindiwe was aghast.

'We met, I think, some years ago at the World Council of Churches' consultation on racism. 1969? My name is Ahmad.'

The old man was shaken, moved. Someone had recognized him.

'I have read your books, of course,' continued Ahmad and, turning to Lindiwe, he said, 'Mr Fortune worked among the hill tribes of India for over twenty years, taught them, helped them, fought their battles with them against the government. Of course he was thrown out. You should read his . . .'

John Fortune had slumped into his chair. He had let the mass of him slacken in a heap. Lindiwe reached out to help him, but he waved her aside. 'Thirty years,' he said, but not in a tone of regret. 'Thirty years,' he repeated, rubbing his hands as though to warm himself in the glow of remembered days. But then there was

Independence and things had begun to change. He had thought he could do missionary work in his own country, but they didn't want people like him any more, they had the police instead. He smiled to himself, a sad smile, wry. There were tears behind his thick glasses somewhere, they had misted over.

'What could be worse,' he asked Ahmad, 'than a missionary without a mission?' And then he smiled that smile of his again and added, 'unless it is a mission without a missionary?'

The following week, Lindiwe came up to Ahmad and put a letter in his hand. 'I am going home to Africa,' she said.